Metaphorosis

May 2023

Beautifully made speculative fiction

Also from Metaphorosis

Metaphorosis Magazine

Metaphorosis: Best of 20xx
Metaphorosis 20xx: The Complete Stories
annual issues, from 2016

Monthly issues

Plant Based Press

Best Vegan Science Fiction & Fantasy
annual issues, 2016-2020

from B. Morris Allen:
Chambers of the Heart: speculative stories
Susurrus
Allenthology: Volume I
Tocsin: and other stories
Start with Stones: collected stories
Metaphorosis: a collection of stories

Verdage

Reading 5X5 x3: Changes
Reading 5X5 x2: Duets
Score – an SFF symphony
Reading 5X5: Readers' Edition
Reading 5X5: Writers' Edition

Vestige

The Nocturnals, by Mariah Montoya

Metaphorosis

May 2023

edited by
B. Morris Allen

ISSN: 2573-136X (online)
ISBN: 978-1-64076-257-2 (e-book)
ISBN: 978-1-64076-258-9 (paperback)

Metaphorosis
a magazine of speculative fiction
from
Metaphorosis Publishing

Neskowin

May 2023

The Diamond Noose

Ramez Yoakeim

From the smug grins everyone flashed me as soon as I walked into the precinct, I knew I was in for a nasty surprise. I hadn't even reached my desk when the lieutenant called me into her glass-bowl office and handed me a new assignment: liaison to the Angels' Embassy.

I didn't care for Angels. They looked down on us from their palaces in the sky, pretending to help us survive our broken world while ensuring we'd never learn to do it on our own. Some said it was the Angels who set off the nuclear catastrophe that nearly wiped out life on Earth.

"Wouldn't this suit a more senior officer?" Or one more junior. Anyone else, really.

The lieutenant jabbed a paper on her desk. "Laila Aboud, requested by name."

A shiver zapped up my spine. The Angels had hidden eyes in the sky, seeing everywhere, knowing all. They had tentacles in every government, in every department, their shadow behind every throne. How had I managed to attract their attention? "Why me?"

She shrugged. "Ask the Angels when you see them. Do we have a problem here?"

I found myself wondering whose idea it had been to call them *Angels*.

"No, ma'am."

Like I had a choice. This job came with a warm bed and three squares, a firearm, and badge that opened doors and dropped eyes. I'd never walk away, no matter what they asked, any more than she would.

After all that, the work was surprisingly mundane. Waiting on my desk every morning was a stack of *requests* from the Angels Embassy: locate knickknacks stolen from the occasional visiting Angel, or quietly deem accidental the death of a prostitute in the company of another, or round up a bunch of uniforms to form a street cordon for visiting off-world dignitaries. Until I arrived at my desk one day to find a single message *requesting* my attendance at the embassy, and my heart dropped to my knees. I wanted to get away from Angels, not get closer.

The embassy occupied an old courthouse downtown. In the frigid gloom under Earth's thick cloud cover, the impeccably restored edifice dwarfed the line of scraggly humanity wrapped around its foundations like a snake about invincible prey.

However the Angels put it, the Transmigration they dangled before those queueing had nothing to do with benevolence. They preyed on our best and brightest, siphoning away those who might help us to break free of our dependence on their conditional aid. Could one of those queuing learn the secrets of fusion one day, or perfect anti-radiation medicines, or discover how to grow crops in poisoned soil, or put an end to the Angels plunder of our water and minerals, or lead us in overthrowing the tyrants they installed to rule us? Not when those with potential got spirited away to the sky.

The queuing adults eyed me warily as I made my way to the uniform separating the line's head from its tail, barring the serpent from becoming an ouroboros. He glanced at my badge and waved me through. Inside, I handed the private security guard my sidearm. "I had no idea they started queueing this early."

"Some never leave." The guard saw me roll my eyes and grinned, his words chasing me to the elevator. "Sometimes, a dream is all that keeps us alive, officer."

A fool's dream of an easy life concerned only with pleasure. Then again, had my lot in life been harsher, perhaps I'd have queued with them.

I wasn't prepared for the mechanical giant waiting for me when the elevator's doors parted. Spindly inside the exoskeleton that afforded her mobility in Earth's gravity, Inspector Geraldine Hoff's skin was as pale as mine was brown, as if we'd been birthed from opposite ends of a monochromatic palette. Her hairless scalp, elongated sloping forehead, and large inky eyes cast as much doubt on our alleged common ancestry as the missing wings myth had it Angels grew to fly around their low-gravity palaces.

While the building's exterior and entrance remained largely faithful to its original layout, the interior bore no resemblance to anything I'd ever seen before. Hoff led me from the lift to a flat-floored ovoid space uniformly lit by the walls themselves. With a whirring flick of her hand, Hoff gestured me towards a blob that oozed up on command and reformed into a stool.

She briefed me on a missing Angel. *The Conjurer* was the nom-de-plume of an artist who composed dreams as a form of entertainment. These visions eschewed euphoric sex or heroic triumph—the sort that'd exhilarate us dirt dwellers—instead, they explored the darker side of the human psyche, torments that Angels no longer experienced. "Any questions?"

I didn't have to ask what the Conjurer was doing on the surface. Where else would he find the human trauma to mine for his *art*? "How does an Angel get lost? No offense, but you stand out down here."

"More reason to suspect something happened to this *Angel*, wouldn't you say?" Hoff bristled at the common moniker. I'd had no idea they considered it pejorative. In their shoes, I'd have been flattered. Would they have preferred us to call them *demons*?

"What exactly do you think I can do that your fancy gizmos can't?"

"Retracing the Conjurer's steps means going places we don't often venture. My bosses, and yours, want a local along to deal with the natives. *No offense.*"

It would've also been politically unpalatable for my bosses to have an undoubtedly armed Angel terrorizing the populace without at least the veneer of local authority, and it didn't hurt to have me around to take the blame when things went awry.

"A chaperone, basically."

Hoff smiled thinly. "Think of it as an opportunity to demonstrate your usefulness."

I didn't know how to respond to *that*.

Mildly acidic drizzle scattered off Hoff's flying egg onto the corroded tin roofs of the lean-tos below. Despite the webbing securing me to the seat, my inner ear kept insisting I was falling towards the transparent shell. White-knuckled, I hung onto the seat and fought off motion sickness, only half-listening to Hoff.

After one particularly sharp banking turn, Hoff glanced at me. "You're turning a worrying shade of green."

I clamped my jaws shut against the rising bile and inflated my lungs with the egg's sweet clean air. "I'm fine."

She pursed her lips and returned her attention to the scarred Earth slipping by below. With little light penetrating the thick, ash-laden clouds, we would all have perished long ago, had it not been for the Angels' magic-like power generation, foodstuffs, and medicines. That their largesse came with strings attached surprised no one. That those strings soon formed a noose that held us hostage to their demands *shouldn't* have surprised anyone.

To shift my focus away from the vertiginous view, I turned to Hoff. "Did the Conjurer stray far during his visits?"

Hoff hesitated. "Sightseeing, entertainment. Nothing out of the ordinary."

She meant poverty safaris and brothels. There was little else for Angels on the surface.

"Could he have gotten lost?" How would the mobs treat a lost Angel? I liked to think some would be hospitable, but I feared that others wouldn't be, and I couldn't bring myself to condemn either.

Hoff shook her head. "He knew his way around." She seemed on the verge of saying more but didn't.

Changing tack, I teased her, "Did you know most people think y'all have wings?"

"Wings?" Hoff frowned back at my smile. "We …" she paused, searching for words, "change bodies like you might clothes. Not as often, but subject to similar whims of fashion and taste. Body parts, like wings or extra eyes or gills and fins, come and go, and are sometimes taken to extremes. Many of my friends forgo bodies entirely to live in the Abstract."

"And that is?"

"Never mind, it's hard to explain." I couldn't tell whether she was boasting or embarrassed.

The egg lurched briefly and I gasped.

Hoff gave me a sidelong glance. "Your file didn't say anything about fear of flying."

I realized I was still holding onto the seat. "I've never flown before, give me time." I tried to let go, but couldn't quite bring myself to do it. "What else did my file say?"

"That you're insubordinate, pigheaded, and cantankerous."

"They could spell *cantankerous*?"

Hoff laughed, and I found myself laughing along, for a moment oblivious to the gulf separating us.

"But it also said you have the highest clearance rate of any officer in your department."

They *had* asked for me by name. I still didn't quite know what to make of that and pushed it aside to ruminate over later.

"Quite the accomplishment, considering how young you are," Hoff added.

I'd never thought of thirty-two as young. Angels were rumored to be immortal, but I put little stock in such claims. If only half of those rumors were true, it would have made them veritable gods. "How old are *you*?"

She smiled coyly and waved away my question. "Longevity's overrated."

"I'd happily part with an arm and both legs to see my fiftieth birthday." With life expectancy in the mid-forties, I found the idea of anyone living to a hundred obscene, let alone longer. How did Angel offspring feel about parents who lingered? Was overpopulation as much of a problem in orbit as it was on the surface?

Hoff stared wistfully into the distance, seeing something in the murky gloom I couldn't. "When life is short, your choices are consequential. Which path you take in life matters more because you only ever get to make a few choices. Live long enough and you end up exploring every path in turn, chasing every dream. What good is success if it's only a matter of time?"

I could tell she sincerely meant it, almost as if she envied me my short miserable life. How easy it was for those well fed to bursting to preach the virtues of restraint to the starving.

Hoff pitched the egg down, drawing my eyes to an expanse of pockmarked, corrugated metal roofs below. Having never seen the area from above before, it took me a moment to recognize where we were. "We can't land here."

"It's the Conjurer's first stop after leaving the embassy. The first deviation from his usual itinerary."

"You don't understand. This is Serpent Head's territory. If we land uninvited, he's as likely to feed us to his dogs as answer our questions."

"I'd like to see him try."

"I wouldn't!" Though I'd count it progress to be rid of him and his flunkies, innocent bystanders were bound to get caught in any confrontation, and for what? To satisfy Hoff's desire to appear tough and powerful? Who was she trying to impress? "You wanted a local to deal with the natives, and this local is telling you to stay the hell away from these natives."

Hoff ignored me and took the egg lower. "I'll land there." She nodded at a stone-paved plaza festooned with tattered bunting and lit with dim, oil-burning lanterns.

By the time the egg touched down, everyone had scattered, leaving the market eerily quiet, aside from the hissing of swaying lamps and the incessant strumming of caustic drizzle on improvised awnings.

"Good luck finding anyone who'll talk to us now," I muttered, steeling myself against the sour miasma wafting through the egg's open hatch.

Hoff gracefully eased the considerable bulk of her exoskeleton out into the open, oblivious to the stench. "They're bound to come out eventually."

"That's not how it works down here, how *we* work," I fumed. Why have me along if she wasn't going to listen to anything I said? "You can't just blunder your way to your missing Conjurer with this confidence act, no matter how convincing."

She cast her eyes down, looking slightly abashed, and I felt a little guilty for my outburst.

I set to scanning the deserted clearing, when a boy bolted from a cart he might have been napping under, towards a dark alley and right into my arms. About ten or twelve, though so thin it was impossible to say for sure, the boy squirmed in my grip, eyes wide with fear.

"Let go, pig," he demanded, his bass rumble at odds with his small frame.

"Settle. I'm not going to hurt you," I said. "There's a half-dinar in it for you if you answer my questions."

The boy stopped bucking and regarded me with wide, greedy eyes. "Ten dinars."

It was a familiar routine. "You don't even know what I'm going to ask you."

Suddenly, floodlights lit the clearing—an extravagant display for a planet starved of power. Reflexively, I let go of the boy's scruff and shielded my eyes. His bare feet barely left a mark on the frozen slush as he ran away.

"Kadir's a good lad. He'd never betray his kin for anything less than *five* dinars." A short, plump man swaggered into view. A tattoo of a snake head in faded indigo and crimson ink covered the left side of his temple, its lean body running down his cheek, under the thicket of a rampant salt-and-pepper beard, and reappearing down the side of his bullneck before disappearing again under his coat's collar. "Are you lost, sweetheart?" Serpent Head asked mockingly. Under the blue-white glare, his shaved head shone like oiled mahogany.

From Hoff's exoskeleton an aura swelled, glowing an ominous red-tinged orange.

Serpent Head regarded her contemptuously. "It's true we have little to live for down here, but believe me, we don't die cheaply." A racket of cocking rifles followed.

"Stop!" I raised my arms. "We didn't come here looking for trouble."

"Trouble?" Serpent Head thundered with practiced menace. "What trouble would that be, sweetheart?"

Hoff covered the distance separating us in a wink. "Call her *sweetheart* one more time and I'll dispatch you like the vermin you are."

Serpent Head matched her advance, his stomping army in lockstep. Instinctively, I stepped in-between. "Enough," I infused my voice with every command authority trick I'd learned walking the beat. "We're only here for information," I continued in a measured tone. "An Angel stopped here a few days ago."

I nodded to Hoff, who asked. "What did he want?"

Serpent Head alternated his focus between my eyes as if one would betray the other. "What's in it for me?"

As soon as he'd finished speaking, Hoff pulled out a small silver box and threw it at him. He grabbed it midair and turned it in his hand, examining it. "What the hell is this?"

"Enough pills to offset five-hundred Sieverts," Hoff said.

I glowered at her. Unlike a coin tossed to a street urchin, bribing Serpent Head with a small fortune in medicine only created a bigger problem. Not that it'd matter to the Angels, not when they had us to clean up their messes.

Serpent Head nodded approvingly at the box. "Your Angel wanted a sedative and—funnily enough—anti-radiation pills. For another one of these," he shook the pills in their container, "I'll tell you where he went next."

"No need." Hoff's forcefield deflated, cooling to a muted indigo-blue as she walked back to the egg, winking out entirely once inside. I scrambled after her. The moment the hatch sealed, the egg shot upwards, pinning me to my seat.

"I could have gotten him to tell us where your Conjurer went next," I grumbled.

"That, I already know."

"Were you planning on telling me?" How could she not understand that to help her, I had to know what I was helping with. Keeping her cards so close to her chest was hurting more than my feelings, it was handicapping our chances of finding the Conjurer. Any investigator worth their salt would've known that. What did Hoff actually do for work up there, parking enforcement?

She saw me glowering and relented. "He went to a bordello, then disappeared without a trace."

So much for Angels eyes seeing everything, knowing all. If an Angel could evade their all seeing eyes, could we too?

One moment, we were drowning in a murky ashen sea, and the next, we burst into an inverted, indigo-hemmed, blue ocean. Against that dazzling expanse, the Angels' crystal palaces glinted like a glittering diamond necklace girding the Earth, an achingly beautiful noose. Despite the blinding brightness, I couldn't turn away, until my eyes watered and reflexively gummed shut. Hoff noticed and polarized the shell into near opacity. "Is this better?"

I watched the fading kaleidoscopic afterimage on the inside of my eyelids, my gratitude for her thoughtfulness warring with resentment. When again would I get a chance to see sunshine, however blinding? For centuries, our leaders had promised a day when the clouds would finally part. Meanwhile, *when-the-sun-shines* had come to mean *never.* "Thank you."

As I reopened my eyes, blinking away the moisture pooling on my lashes, a nagging feeling I had since we took off from the marketplace coalesced into a question. "Why did the Conjurer buy radiation pills on the black market? Unlike yours, the local ones are useless as currency."

"Currency?" Hoff scolded. "Is that the gratitude we get for helping you survive?"

"You want *our* gratitude for exploiting us?" I responded in kind. "Everything you do, you do for yourselves. Every time you bribe someone like Serpent Head, you strengthen his hand and ensure generations of Kadirs never rise to challenge your interests."

"If you're going to blame us for Serpent Head, you have to ask yourself this: Why would we bother sabotaging your endeavors when you do such a fine job of it on your own? Everything you accuse us of, Laila, you are yourself complicit in."

I smarted from the truth.

Hoff broke the silence that ensued. "Must we quarrel about things that have nothing to do with the two of us? I don't blame you for every fault of your people. Why blame me for mine?"

"Because you have a say. You get to vote on the decisions your people make. *You* decide what's right and what's not. I don't. I live and die by the edicts of the tyrants you installed as our rulers. How our troubles started may not have been your fault, but we're still in a mess, centuries later, because it serves your interests. You use us, Geraldine."

"Can't we . leave politics to the politicians?"

"Why am I here, Geraldine? And don't give me this bullshit about locals and natives. You don't listen to anything I say anyway. There's nothing I've done you couldn't have done on your own."

"You're wrong, Laila." Hoff paused and regarded me diffidently, before continuing. "Back home, there are no hardships, no risks. We've forgotten pain, fear, hunger. When we set out to rid ourselves of human weakness, we ended up discarding our instincts instead. You effortlessly saw through my bravado in the face of the first hitch we faced. I'm overwhelmed by your world and woefully unprepared for it. I can't finish this on my own."

She'd called me by my first name twice now. A sincere familiarity, or another manipulation? I couldn't tell. Then I realized that I too had called her by her first name. Was I trying to manipulate her in return, or had I simply forgotten she was an Angel?

"Then tell me why the Conjurer needed anti-radiation pills, when his aura would've protected him as yours protects you," I paused for a response, but Hoff only shrugged. "You said your people choose their bodies. Could he have chosen a body that is susceptible to radiation?"

Hoff's eyes glazed over for a heartbeat or two. "It's not. His current corpus is an older model than mine, but similarly immune to radiation. Curiously, though, he hasn't upgraded his for nearly twenty years."

"The same period he's been visiting the surface, give or take?"

Hoff turned towards me so fast, I recoiled, driving my head deeper into the headrest. "How did you know that?"

"My guess is, the Conjurer wasn't born an Angel."

"No one is born—" Hoff stopped mid-sentence. "—into Transenlightenment."

"You don't have kids?" I'd never even heard a rumor about that. I wouldn't have believed it had anyone else told me. How could a people survive without having offspring? "Why not?"

Hoff shook her head. "You first. How did you work all this out?"

"If the Conjurer didn't need the pills, then they had to be for one of us, for someone he knew. Had he sourced them the way you had, you'd have a record of it. Maybe he wouldn't have been able to explain why he needed them or for whom." I paused, giving Hoff another opportunity to tell me I was wrong. She said nothing. "Circumventing obstacles and challenging limits is something we have to do, dozens of times every day, just to survive. But you just said those sorts of instincts are lost to you, which would make the Conjurer a more recent Angel. One who hadn't yet shed his hard-won survival instincts. One who still has people here he cares enough about to risk doing business with the likes of Serpent Head. Who is it? After twenty years, his parents are likely dead. A lover then, or a child?"

Hoff's response was slow coming. "I don't know."

I snorted and turned away from her, shaking my head.

"We don't keep those sorts of records. We never had to," she added heatedly. After a pause, she drew in a deep breath before continuing. "To answer your earlier question, the longevity treatments preclude pregnancy. We could have found ways around that, but at some point we decided we didn't want to, and however long we live, we too die. So, we invite the deserving among you to join us. We expect and accept a measure of nostalgia for their former lives, until new possibilities sets them free of their past. Why would we need records of their old lives?"

I thought of the coiling queue outside the embassy and shivered. Did those queuing know the price of becoming an Angel was to give up everyone they'd ever loved? "You expect a spouse to forget their mate, a parent to abandon their children, a friend and neighbor to forswear their community after a *measure of nostalgia*?"

She shrugged. "I don't remember what family I once had, or even if I had one."

Where did she think she'd come from, a seed pod? All humans had families, born or found, small or sprawling, loving or venom-filled. They might not like them or want them, but they had them. Whom had the Conjurer left behind twenty years ago? How long had it taken Hoff to forgot those she'd abandoned? "Geraldine, why are you searching for the Conjurer? The truth, please."

"He took something he shouldn't have."

I waited for her to elaborate, but that was all she would say.

After Serpent Head's hostile reception, Madam Sparrow's solicitous guards seemed downright hospitable. They ushered us through the darkened brothel to their mistress's alcove in the back where she fussed over a young woman's makeup.

Madam Sparrow watched our approach with naked appraisal. A firm hand to the small of the back propelled the young woman towards us. Midstride, her heel caught on the tail of her two-sizes too-long dress and she tripped. Hoff caught her before she face-planted, and helped her back to her feet. "How old are you, child?"

Madam Sparrow leered at Hoff, answering before the young woman could, "Old enough. You could be her first."

Hoff wrinkled her nose. "Revolting. Inhuman."

I bridled at Hoff's patronizing self-righteousness, especially coming from someone who'd remorselessly sacrificed her family, even their memory. "At least she's warm, well-fed, and has somewhere dry to lay her head at night. So long as no one's forcing her, I have no quarrel with her choices." I turned to Madam Sparrow. "We're not customers. We're looking for an Angel who visited your establishment a few days ago."

"I have no idea who you're talking about." Up close, grey roots peeked from under the edges of Madam Sparrow's platinum-blonde wig.

"I can think of a few ways to jog your memory, none of them good for business."

Madam Sparrow glowered at me, but eventually her rounded shoulders slumped, the fire in her eyes replaced by a heavy weariness that could flatten mountains. "I don't know where he went, alright? Years ago, before he left to become an Angel, he brought his woman here. Paid well for her upkeep too, and she doted on the girls like the children they never had. Every few weeks, he'd visit for a day or two. This time, he took her and left."

Hoff shook her head. "No, he didn't. He entered through your front door and never left."

Madam Sparrow bobbed her head coyly. "Not by the front door, no."

Hoff had to fold her frame at the waist to fit into the back door's antechamber. Behind the raised hem of a faded wall tapestry, the tunnel's mouth was pitch black. Narrow and low-ceilinged, it swallowed my pocket torch's beam, dispersing it without illuminating its confines.

"Where does it lead?" Hoff asked Madam Sparrow.

"The woods, an hour on foot south of town."

The hairs on my nape bristled. "The haunted woods?"

Hoff sighed audibly. "It's not haunted."

Madam Sparrow put her hands on her hips. "Haunted or not, some *very* important clients rely on this tunnel's discretion," she cautioned, her emphasis leaving me in no doubt she meant Angels. "Compromise it at your peril." With a huff, she turned and left.

"The woods are only mildly radioactive, but that's enough to turn them into a blind spot for our orbital sensors. I should have thought of that when we couldn't locate him." Hoff peered into the tunnel. "Did you want to go first or should I?"

"After you, but it's quite narrow. You might get stuck."

"The injury to my dignity would be far worse, if we were to fail."

We emerged from the side of a low hill into a dense thicket of dead poplars lumbering side by side like funereal guards. Their naked branches sagged under the accumulated snow. A burden which the chilling wind forced them to shed periodically, obscuring whatever tracks our quarry might have left.

Hoff deposited a blue pill in my hand. "Take this."

My eyes fixed on the tiny pill. "Trust is a two way street, Geraldine." Somehow, unconsciously, Angel Inspector Geraldine

Hoff had become merely Hoff, my partner, and my partner Hoff had morphed into my friend, Geraldine. I expected commensurately more from her. "I've trusted you plenty so far. I got into your flying egg having never flown before, jumped between you and Serpent Head to stave off disaster, and threatened Sparrow to find your Conjurer. Now's your turn."

"There're things you don't need to know. But I never deceived you."

"In a true partnership, you don't get to decide what I need to know. That's something you do with an underling. Prove to me I'm not just a useful dirt dweller to use and discard."

Hoff held my stare unblinkingly for a few heartbeats before relenting. "What do you want to know?"

I closed my fingers around the pill to steady my shaking hand. "What did the Conjurer steal?"

"It's not what you think," Hoff said quietly, her voice barely audible over the wind whistling through dead branches. "The nanites he stole protect the newly transmigrated from the perils of life in orbit—cellular damage caused by cosmic radiation, bone loss, cardiovascular irregularities—until they're ready for new bodies immune to those problems."

I popped the pill into my mouth and swallowed. It left a bitter aftertaste. "What else are you not telling me?"

Hoff ignored me and marched off into the faintly luminescent forest in a cloud of mechanical noises.

We searched the forest on foot, our progress punctuated by the wheezing and whistling wind, the concert of Hoff's exoskeleton, and the crunches and squishes of rotting debris and frozen twigs in the snow-covered underbrush.

Hoff peered into the darkness, seeing what no human eye could. Midstride, she grabbed my arm and whispered, "Thermal gradient ahead."

A hundred meters later, we glimpsed a log cabin nestled in a copse of dead cedars. Its roof sagged under accumulated snow and a muted orange glow spilled from between the planks of its boarded windows.

"He's here, the Conjurer. This close, I can detect his exoskeleton," Hoff said. "Please wait here. I don't know if he's armed, and I can't neutralize him and protect you at the same time." She didn't wait for me to respond, and started trudging through the snow towards the cabin's back door.

Every time I thought I'd peeled back her last façade, Hoff surprised me with another shell inside. Secrets within secrets, manipulations masquerading as truths. Whether there was someone I'd recognize as human at the core of that matryoshka doll, I didn't know, but I was done trusting. I had to see for myself.

The moment Hoff moved out of sight, I set off towards the front of the cabin and didn't stop until I'd mounted the low-rise porch's warped wooden steps and peeked inside. The cabin was dark beyond a circle of light shed by a flameless lantern of an unfamiliar design set on the floor. Facing it was an Angel in an exoskeleton, not unlike Hoff's, sitting on his haunches by a pile of soiled rags. The door creaked when I pushed it open and the Conjurer looked up at me.

I'd seen that all-too-human vacant gaze of despair before. In the eyes of a mother cradling the lifeless body of her starved infant, or a child staring uncomprehending at the remains of his parents on a pyre. Crying tearlessly and swaying gently to a morose tune only the bereaved could hear, an insistent yet futile attempt at self-soothing.

The Conjurer's blood-smeared fingers trembled, every flutter amplified by his exoskeleton. As I approached, the mess on the floor resolved to a vague human outline that had somehow been turned inside out. The stench caught in my throat like a punch to the gut. I bent to the side and retched.

He muttered something, repeating it at the threshold of audibility. I wiped my mouth on the back of my cold hand and leaned closer as Hoff walked in through the back door.

Dazed, the Conjurer moaned endlessly, "I killed her. I killed her."

I sat on the porch steps, lost in thought and breathing hard to purge the stench from my nose. The more I thought about it, the more I realized it was the Conjurer's raw grief that unmoored me. It was all too human. Was it only the newly transmigrated who retained these shadows of their former self? How long before even those echoes faded? Did Hoff feel anything at all anymore, and if not, was she still human?

When the porch floorboards creaked behind me, I summoned my composure with hurried gulps of frigid air, brushed the freezing moisture off my cheeks, and looked up to find Hoff standing over me. "What'll become of him?"

"He stole restricted technology and inflicted great harm with it. That love motivated him won't excuse his transgression."

"He couldn't have known it'd kill her." I felt sure any punishment the Angels had in store would pale next to his loss.

Hoff bobbed her head, the gesture both oppressively familiar and discomfiting in its otherness. "The nanites are lethal when administered under gravity. Instead of healing her ills, they unraveled her body at a molecular level. They were never meant for surface dwellers. He should've known better."

I nodded, not because I agreed, but because I could imagine how he felt. He hadn't wanted the wife the Angels had rejected to die alone. He either hadn't known the nanites would be lethal on the surface or hadn't believed it. Who could blame him, after a life filled of Angel half-truths and outright lies? I figured becoming an Angel himself wasn't enough to erase that ingrained suspicion we all shared of our sky-dwelling exploiters and benefactors.

I pulled myself up and brushed the snow off my clothes, puzzled at how dry and warm Hoff appeared inside her protective cage.

We both stood staring into the darkness, taking in both the darkness we faced and that behind us. Hoff broke the spell, speaking softly, barely louder than the whistling wind and shivering branches. "Wish we'd met under better circumstances. Still, we make quite the team, you and I."

I smiled a little at that, having no idea what other circumstance she imagined would have brought an Angel and someone like me together. "Until the next time one of yours goes missing, then."

"It doesn't have to be. *Inspector Laila Aboud* has a certain ring to it, don't you think?"

I groaned. "Please tell me all of this wasn't just a recruitment test."

Geraldine shook her head, the exoskeleton straining like a laden truck attempting a steep hill. She reached out an arm and the exoskeleton peeled back, blooming around her hands. Her skin was warm and soft against my frigid hands. "Must you suspect every motive, distrust everyone?"

"Occupational hazard, I'm afraid." *Not to mention your duplicitous manipulations*, I thought to myself, but held my tongue.

"Well? Would you like to become an *Angel*?" Hoff said, as if proposing, hastening to add with a slight nod towards the cabin, "The proper way."

"It's a big leap to leave everyone and everything I know behind."

Hoff bobbed her head. "It's not obligatory. In time, your priorities will change. Your past will fade into the deepest recesses of your memory, until it's beyond recall. It works out for the best in the end."

"It didn't for the Conjurer."

"And see where it led him."

I shook my head. Angels were a cautionary tale, not a model to emulate. No matter how hard they tried, they'd never be truly human again. *We* had to survive if there were to be humans walking the Earth in another thousand years.

Hoff smirked a little. "You're telling me you've never thought about it?"

Gently, I reclaimed my hands from Geraldine's and shoved them into my pockets. "I don't think there's anyone who hasn't, but fantasizing with my feet planted firmly on the ground is not the same as throwing it all away to chase the unknown." I was sorely tempted to say yes, if for no other reason than for a chance to see that diamond noose again. to revel in its brilliance before, left unchecked, it choked the life out of our species.

"You won't regret it, trust me."

Hoff's palpable excitement left me unsure how she'd react if I flatly declined. "Could I think about it?"

Despite the puzzled surprise etched on her face, Hoff's smile lingered. "Take as long as you need."

I nodded and looked away, my eyes drawn upwards to the starless darkness enveloping the Earth. I knew I'd never belong up there, any more than the Conjurer had. I belonged to the earth. To those used and forgotten. I didn't count myself one of Earth's best or brightest; I'd never be a fusion physicist or a horticulturist, or even a revolutionary, but perhaps, when the time came, I could do my small part.

See Ramez Yoakeim's story "The Diamond Noose" online at Metaphorosis.
If you liked it, leave a comment. Authors love that!
Remember to subscribe to our e-mail updates so you'll know when new stories are posted.

About the story

The core idea came from a news report about proposed changes to immigration selection criteria, basing it more on skills and qualifications and less on family connections. I started thinking about what that meant for those selected in their new foreign homes, for those they leave behind, and for the people who yield their best and brightest to other invariably more affluent and powerful people. I relied on my personal experience as the child of immigrants and an immigrant myself later in life to navigate what proved to be a complex dilemma.

A question for the author

Q: What is your favourite part of writing?

A: When I'm writing, anything is possible, including giving this instinctive introvert a voice extending far beyond anything achievable on my own. It's also a sort of therapy as I inhabit a multitude of characters, each with their own backstories, perspectives, and conflicts, and in so doing discover otherwise inaccessible nuances of human motivation. Lastly, what better escapism from the present with its threats of war and cataclysm than the future, not because that future will necessarily be any better (we can hope, but then again we have history), but because then, at least in our imagination, humanity has any future at all!

About the author

Born in Egypt, raised in Australia, and now living with his husband in the United States, Ramez Yoakeim spent his whole life adapting. A one-time engineer and educator, Ramez's work favors the darker side of SFF but mostly he writes about hope.

yoakeim.com, @RamezYoakeim

The Conch Shell

Elizabeth Raphael

Mira sat on the couch, clutching the conch shell tightly in her hands. Her back had gone stiff and her legs were sweating against the soft leather of the couch, but she dared not move—not yet. If she stayed there just a little longer, she told herself, surely she would remember why she was holding the shell. Despite everything, she still had faith in the power of her mind. All she needed to do was focus, and with a bit of time, it all would fall into place. She took several slow breaths, the kind she had learned in the yoga class that Thalia insisted she take, and waited for the moment to return to her. It did not.

Mira let out a breath in a huff, the loops of her ever-present pearl necklace clinking softly against each other with the motion. She had never been one to wallow in self-pity, but she could feel it now, coiling itself around her body and threatening to pull her down. Her late husband had once told her that her ability to find the smallest sliver of positivity in any situation was a big part of what made him fall for her, but at the moment, she felt far removed from that version of herself. She could see no silver lining to dementia. She was being stolen away, piece by piece, and there was nothing she could do about it. Logically, she knew it was an indiscriminate condition, but the raw emotional side of her still wanted to throw herself to the ground like a toddler having a tantrum and wail about the unfairness of it all. She had done everything right, everything that was supposed to ensure that she aged as gracefully as possible. She had eaten a balanced diet, enjoying her food but not overindulging—or, rather, over-indulging only on special occasions. She had stayed physically active, swimming a daily mile until her early sixties, when arthritis seized her shoulders and she was forced to switch to walking. She had never been as graceful on land as in the water, but she had taken to walking regardless. As long as she was up and active, she was happy.

The cruelest bit of all, or so it felt to her, was that she had been just as diligent with her cognitive health. In addition to her daily crossword, she periodically took up disparate hobbies so she'd gain diverse skills—everything from archery to rangoli. She had walked through life with a tenacious optimism that everything would turn out OK, and it hadn't.

Fighting off a wave of despair, Mira tightened her grip on the shell. She knew it was risky to stay in this pose. That new helper of hers—Kylee, Mira recalled after only a brief hesitation, Kylee with a double 'e' at the end—was due any minute now. If Kylee came in and saw Mira frozen like this, she would immediately call Thalia to let her know that her mother was having another episode. Thalia would then leave work straight away and drive the nearly 100 miles that separated them, likely using that time to work on a new pitch for persuading Mira to move into a retirement home.

Mira's mouth twisted at the thought. Thalia was too young to fully understand the situation. To her, it was simple: Mira's dementia was progressing—a fact that Mira herself could not deny—and therefore, she shouldn't live alone. Why not be part of a community full of people who were going through the same sort of thing, cared for by workers trained for that very purpose? Mira shook her head. How easy it was for Thalia to come to such conclusions when it wasn't her being forced to leave the home she had lived in for nearly 60 years. It wasn't her being expected to leave behind the living room where her child had taken her first steps, the library full of her carefully curated books, swimming trophies, and assorted treasures, the bedroom that she had shared with her husband for 54 wonderful, too-short years. No, it certainly wasn't Thalia's freedom and privacy being stripped bare. It wasn't her world being compressed down into one personality-devoid room.

Mira's pulse thrummed an angry staccato inside of her, each beat a warning. She had to stop getting angry like this, she chastised herself. It wasn't good for her, and it wasn't fair to Thalia.

Thalia's single-mindedness could be frustrating, true, but she was a good woman and a good daughter. She was just a worrier, as her father had been. There was no ill intent behind this retirement home crusade of hers, Mira knew; there was only love. Thalia had harbored concerns about Mira living alone after her father's passing, and Mira's short-lived disappearance six months back had unfortunately given meat to those fears. If Thalia didn't have to travel so often for work, she undoubtedly would have cleared out a bedroom in her condo and convinced Mira to move in long ago. As matters stood, this was her way of trying to keep Mira safe.

A cell phone trilled loudly from the coffee table, interrupting Mira's line of thought. Prying a hand from the shell, she slid her turquoise reading glasses down in place from the top of her head and leaned over, squinting at the name flashing across the small screen. It was Thalia. A smile quirked Mira's mouth. It was almost as if Thalia had sensed Mira's train of thought and waited until she meandered into a more positive frame of mind to call. Thalia had always been an intuitive child.

Mira picked up the phone with her free hand. "Hello, dear," she said, her back popping as she leaned back against the couch. "I was just thinking about you."

"Hey, hey. How's my favorite mother today?" There was a faintly echoey quality to Thalia's voice, which told Mira that she was on speaker phone. That was not unusual. Thalia was usually doing at least ten things at once. At the beginning of her daughter's career, Mira had been surprised by how busy the life of a marine biologist was, but she was well used to it at this point.

"Your favorite mother is fine." Mira supposed that was a partial truth. Her eyes flicked towards the mahogany grandfather clock that stood solemnly in the corner. "It's early for a call from you. Late lunch?"

Thalia clicked her tongue, a nervous gesture that had started when she was around eight. Nowadays, it indicated that Thalia was particularly worried about Mira's health. "No, Mom," Thalia began carefully. "I'm leaving on my trip to Mexico today. We got the grant to go to Lake Xochimilco and study the axolotls. I'll be gone for a month."

Mira muttered several choice curses inside her head—phrases that Thalia would have been shocked to hear, had they actually slipped out of her mother's mouth. "I know all of that, Thalia," she lied. "I just thought you left tomorrow."

There was a brief, weighted pause. "Oh. Yeah. This trip has been such a long time in the making, it is hard to believe it's finally here." A horn honked faintly in the background. "Ugh—this traffic." Thalia tsked. "I thought by leaving early, I'd get ahead of it all."

"It's tourist season. Rush hour is every hour."

Thalia snorted. "That's true. So"—her voice took on a tone of practiced ease —"how are you doing today?"

"You already asked that, love."

"I know, I'm just..." Thalia clicked her tongue. "I applied for this grant before everything happened, and it's such a long trip. I don't know. Maybe it's not the right time."

"Thalia—" Mira tried to interject, but Thalia seemed not to hear her.

"I'd like to be there to get things going, so I could always go and then leave after a week or two. Dr. Slater is more than qualified to handle everything on his own.

Well, on his own with all of the research assistants. He'd be fine. I'm superfluous, really."

"THALIA," Mira's voice was loud and firm. "You are not now, nor have you ever been superfluous. This trip has been your dream since you were a child, and it's your hard work that made it happen. You will go on this trip, all four weeks of it, and you won't think of me at all while you're there. That's final."

"Oh, Mom." Mira could hear the smile in Thalia's voice. "How could I not think of you? If it weren't for you, I wouldn't be a marine biologist. You taught me everything I know."

"Ohh, pshh," Mira said dismissively, just as her cheeks flushed with pleasure. "I think your professors probably did that."

"Not really. You knew that the Greenland shark was the oldest vertebrate over the bowhead whale before that research was even published. That bit really impressed my 'Intro to Marine Bio' class. I think Professor Gruber thought I was a witch," Thalia laughed. "Though witchcraft is as good of an explanation as any. Your knowledge of the ocean has always bordered on the supernatural."

"I read a lot of books, love. That's hardly supernatural."

"True, but that doesn't fully explain—"

"So," Mira interrupted, pivoting the conversation. There was an explanation, she knew, but of course she couldn't remember what it was. Thalia didn't need to know that, though. "You mentioned that a Dr. Slater will be on this trip. Is he that handsome British fellow we ran into at that Cuban restaurant?"

"He is," Thalia answered suspiciously.

"He's the one with the wife and three daughters, right?"

"Hmm—no, Dr. Slater is single. I'm not sure who you're thinking of," Thalia said before picking up on her mother's comfortingly familiar matchmaking attempt. "Oh, wait. I see what you did there. I tripped right into that one."

Mira smiled. "Your old mother still has a few tricks. I know you'll be busy on this trip, but hey, there's a lot of hours in the day."

"Duly noted." Thalia clicked her tongue. "So you're really all right? Really? I worry about you all alone."

"I won't be alone. I have Kylee, I have that yoga class—I'll be fine."

"But you seemed fine before your disappearance." Thalia took a deep breath. "You know, Coastal Gardens is really more of an apartment complex than a retirement home. You'd have your own space—"

"I'll be fine. That's not going to happen again," Mira said, willing her voice to sound more assured than she felt.

Thalia clicked her tongue. "OK, mom. I'll still have my cell. So you can call me, and I'll call you, of course. Let's see... " Thalia drummed her fingers on the steering wheel. "My itinerary is on your fridge, but I'll text it to Kylee so she has it, too." She clicked her tongue. "I guess that's everything."

"Have a good trip, love."

"Bye, mom. I'm only a phone call away if you need me for anything. I love you."

"Love you, too."

The smile slowly faded from Mira's face as she set her cell back down and wrapped her freed hand back around the shell. Her disappearance. It always came back to that. It was a specter that she could never escape from, one determined to wreck her past and present. There had been mental lapses before then, but that blasted episode was when it really became a problem. Cruelest of all, the events of that day remained a mystery.

Familiar feelings of frustration and fear rose in Mira as she once again tried to remember what had happened the day of her disappearance. She had eaten her usual breakfast—soft-boiled egg on a piece of wheat toast—then dressed in her exercise clothes and set out for her daily walk. After that, she recalled nothing. Nothing until nearly two days later, when she was found on a beach nearly 65 miles away by a group of early morning surfers, soaking wet but otherwise fine.

Shades of that day occasionally came to her. They bore no true form but gave an overall feeling of peace. However she had gotten there and whatever she had been doing, she had not been afraid. The fear had come later, when she was being subjected to every test possible in the hospital. On the beach, she had felt safe.

Mira sat up straight, scooting to the edge of the couch. The beach. That day. That's when she had gotten the conch shell, wasn't it? Yes, she realized with sudden clarity, excitement buzzing through her. She had argued with the EMTs—they hadn't wanted her to bring it in the ambulance—but Mira had refused to get in without it. She kept insisting she had found it, it was important, and she wasn't going to give it up.

But no, that wasn't quite right, was it? Mira's nails drummed against the rough exterior of the shell as she thought. That was what she had told the EMTs, but she had already started to forget by then, hadn't she? Forget that she had not found it; it had been given to her. Yes, that was it! It had been given to her by someone she knew, someone she loved, someone she had not seen in a long time. Mira's right leg bounced in time to the drumming of her fingers as the moment solidified further. She could almost picture their face, but the image was distorted, as if viewed through a warped mirror.

The front door burst open in a flurry of noise and motion. Mira reflexively leapt to her feet, nearly dropping the shell in the process. A small blonde woman—Kylee— stepped through the entranceway a few seconds after.

"Sorry, sorry!" Kylee said, bowing her head in apology. "That wind is nuts! The storm must be coming sooner than they said." She shut the door behind her with visible effort. "That door got away from me."

"So it would seem!" Mira's voice was faint, her heart still pounding from the surprise.

Kylee quickly finger-combed her windblown tresses and pulled the hair back into a low ponytail, securing it with a black scrunchie that she slid off of her wrist. "Your doorbell is broken, by the way. I was out there ringing it for, like, five minutes."

Mira chose to avoid the obvious question as to why Kylee didn't just knock on the door. Instead, she tsked in sympathy.

"I told Thalia I didn't need one of those camera bells. The more fancy parts an item has, the more likely they are to break."

Kylee slung her purse down on the coffee table. "No biggie—I'll just give that handyman of yours a call. Hopefully he'll be able to come out soon and do some troubleshooting. Is his card still on the fridge?"

"Should be." Mira settled herself back down on the couch.

"Good. I'll put on a pot of coffee while I'm in there. After being tossed about in that wind, I could use a warming up. Want a cup?"

"Mmm—add a splash of chocolate milk to mine."

Kylee raised her brows. "Oh, that sounds good! I'll have to try it, too." She gestured towards Mira's lap. "Cool shell, by the way! Doing some dusting?"

"Oh!" Mira looked down. She had forgotten that she had been holding the conch. "I was...admiring it." That was right, wasn't it?

"I can see why. It's a beauty!" Kylee reached out and stroked the smooth inner curve of the shell. "Look at those colors— just like a sunrise! When I was 10, my aunt went deep-sea fishing off the coast of the Florida Keys and brought me back one of these. She ate the conch, and I got the shell. I thought it was the prettiest thing in the world—almost as pretty as yours. Anyway, it broke during a move just two years after I got it. Military life, you know? I was crushed. It was the star of my shell collection." The corners of Kylee's mouth turned down ever so slightly, an odd sight on her normally impossibly cheerful face.

A pang of sympathy struck Mira. She knew that to most, Kylee's story would seem inconsequential. But as a woman with more than one collection, she knew it to be quite serious, indeed.

Mira patted Kylee's hand. "I'm sorry about that, dear." Mira took care to make sure that her tone sounded serious and respectful.

Kylee met Mira's eyes and flashed a grateful smile. "Thanks. You know what's silly? Every night before bed—when I still had the shell, obviously—I used to hold it up to my ear so I could hear the ocean. I'd sit there like that for at least five minutes." She chuckled. "That's funny—I haven't thought about that in forever. I was an odd kid. Memories..."

Kylee shook her head, amused with herself, then disappeared into the kitchen.

"Memories," Mira echoed in a voice barely loud enough to even be considered a whisper.

Mira waited until she heard the coffee pot start bubbling and the murmur of Kylee chatting with the handyman before she began. Supporting the shell with both hands, she raised it up with a slow reverence and placed it carefully against her ear.

Mira gasped. At the sound of the soft woosh from inside the shell, it all came back—who she really was, where she'd really come from. She remembered her whole life, which had begun beneath the waves. Warm and weightless, she would ride the currents and tides, powered by the undulation of her tail.

Oh, her tail! It had been beautiful, a glistening gradient of blue and green scales that melded seamlessly with the soft, pliable skin at her waist. Her family all had the same colors on their tails, though arranged in different patterns.

Oh! She had a family down there—a large family! Parents, six sisters, and four times as many aunts, uncles, and cousins. She had loved them fiercely, and they had loved her in return. It had broken her heart to leave them behind, but she had known then, deep in the marrow of her bones, that part of her destiny lay on the land. As with the other mermaids who had made the choice before her, she had been granted the opportunity to leave the water with the understanding that when her human form was nearing its end, she would return it and her soul to the sea. Far from being an unwelcome caveat, she had taken comfort in the knowledge that some day, she would return.

Mira gasped yet again as it all connected. That day, her disappearance— she had not had an episode. She had been called to that beach! One of her sisters—Adria, beautiful Adria with the long black hair that curled like no one else's in their family—had been waiting there in the waters for her. She had aged at approximately one quarter of the rate that Mira had on land, but it was the kindness radiating from Adria that truly made her beautiful. Mira would have been content just to gaze upon her sister again, but Adria had called her there to give her an important gift—the shell. Not just an object of beauty, it was a talisman designed to help bring Mira back to herself.

Tears pooled in the corner of Mira's mouth as they streamed down her face, their salty taste carrying with it the echoes of the sea. Her heart bloomed with a joy beyond words. She had lost much over the years, and she knew that even this moment might soon slip away from her.

But right now, she remembered.

See Elizabeth Raphael's story "The Conch Shell" online at Metaphorosis.

*If you liked it, leave a comment. Authors love
that!
Remember to subscribe to our e-mail updates so
you'll know when new stories are posted.*

About the story

I often write either to escape reality or process it, and with "The Conch Shell", it turned out to be a bit of both. My grandmother, who served as inspiration for this story, has late stage Alzheimer's. She has sadly forgotten most of her life, but odd fragments come through, often paradoxically. For example, she doesn't remember having children or grandchildren, but she remembers being at my wedding. This got me thinking about the significance of what moments in our lives stick with us, and the pain that comes with forgetting.

At its core, "The Conch Shell" is an exploration of aging and memory. Older people are too often marginalized by society, and this is magnified when the person has dementia. In creating the character of Mira, I aimed to put the voice, and a bit of dignity, back where it belonged.

Though Mira's journey is unique to her situation, there is a wider truth that I hope comes across. Whether from dementia or the chaos of life, it is all too easy to lose bits of yourself. Some parts may be impossible to regain, but others will come back to you if you just reach out and grab them. And maybe, just maybe, what you get back will be magic.

A question for the author

Q: What is the first/most recent book that you lost sleep reading/thinking about?

A:　I have a vivid imagination and an obsessive personality so I frequently lose sleep over books, but one of my most memorable reads so far this year is *Hell Bent*, the second book in Leigh Bardugo's *Alex Stern* series. Much like the first book, *Ninth House*, *Hell Bent* manages to be equal parts thought-provoking and positively bonkers. It's an unflinching look at class, gender, and racial conflict. It's an exploration of the transformative power of trauma. It shines a light at the darkness that lies within us all. It does all of that, while also having naked demons, ghosts, frat boy vampires, and other similarly attention-grabbing plot devices and twists. I laughed, I cried, I said 'whaaaat' and 'nooooo' outloud to myself several times while reading. Truly, *Hell Bent* is a standard-setting masterpiece of dark academia.

About the author

Elizabeth Raphael enjoys arranging letters in pleasing patterns. She is most at peace in libraries and bookstores, where she whittles away many moments gazing wordlessly uponst ink on pages. In writing as in reading she dabbles in many genres, but speculative fiction has her heart.

ElizabethRaphael.com

Anamnesis

Karl El-Koura

At first she thought the white cloud floating across the blue sky had an interesting shape, almost like the face of a man.

Her head resting on her intertwined fingers, Allie lay stretched out on her long beach towel, which had been imprinted with multicolored stars and nebulae against black space. She let her gaze drift to the sun, so bright and beautifully yellow, then down to her friend Marcia.

"What's that thing called," Allie said, "when you see something that looks human?"

Marcia had been posing, more than relaxing, her torso lifted on her elbows, one leg drawn up; trying to catch the eye of the boys chasing the waves while pretending she didn't notice them. She shrugged, but answered: "Pareidolia."

Allie nodded, then returned her gaze languidly up the sky, back to the cumulus cloud. Except it wasn't just vaguely suggestive of human features anymore. She sat up. The cloud had taken definite shape; as if some cosmic god had stuck his nose into the mist, which had molded around his face.

"Marcia," she said, pointing. "Look."

Reluctantly Marcia tore her gaze off the muscular boys. "I don't see anything," she said, then began to hum.

"What are you—?" The rest of the question died on Allie's lips. The tune reminded her of something. Of someone? "What song is that?" she said finally.

Marcia stared. "What song?"

"The one you were humming just now."

"I wasn't." And then, as if the question had reminded her of it, Marcia took up the tune once more, the melody beginning again in her throat, escaping through her closed mouth.

Allie shut her eyes, tried to place the melody. After a few minutes, her mind refusing to give up the answer despite, or perhaps because of the forcefulness of her concentration, she opened her eyes again and set aside that puzzle for the moment to focus on another: the face in the cloud. The oval shape, the dimpled chin, the thin lips, the protruding arrow of a nose, the round eyes a little too close to each other, the thick eyebrows and bald head.

"I know him," she said.

Marcia stopped humming long enough to say "Who?" and then resumed the song.

The answer was there, but just beyond her mental reach. She could sense it, like something tucked away in a closet she couldn't open. "I'm going home," she said, standing.

Still propped up on her elbows, Marcia stopped humming, said, "Okay," then began the song again.

Allie bent over to pick up her towel, but realization broke through: *my God, it's a lullaby.*

Had someone sung it to her as a baby?

Now that she tried, though, she realized with rising panic that she couldn't remember, not that far back …

and not anything at all, as if a shroud had been cast over her memories.

"Marcia, I don't feel so good," she said, before she fell forward ... and fell and fell, because the hard, gravelly sand wasn't there to catch her. Instead she tumbled into one of the black empty spaces of her towel, slipping past the interstellar clouds, distant stars rising around her like columns of fire ... falling and falling in the endless void until she lost consciousness.

By developing a strict daily routine, Andrick Peret had been able to hold the loneliness at bay for almost a year.

First, he had to finish his breakfast before he allowed himself to check the distress signal. That early morning sliver of time was the second best part of his day, and it wasn't because the coffee (forbidden for so long) was delicious, better than any he'd ever had, or that he had his pick of a wide assortment of flash-frozen, vacuum-sealed breakfasts to choose from—sliced fruit, eggs soft- and hard-boiled, sausages, pancakes, waffles, all kinds of syrups and jams. After several weeks, even delicious food became commonplace; the novelty of popping off a tab and watching the coffee or food instantly heat up as air rushed in became routine even more quickly. No, he cherished that small stretch of time because he could eat his breakfast while anticipating the possibility that he'd walk into the small control room and find the blinking light had changed color.

Very soon after the crash, he'd created a subroutine that beamed out an SOS every hour, providing their location and status, and he'd wired it so that if a response came in at any point, a light on the dashboard would turn from red to green. A blinking green light meant that someone had acknowledged their signal throughout the night; maybe someone on their way to rescue them.

Every morning for eleven months, however, Andrick continued to see the light blinking the red distress color even before he'd entered the control room, its glow seeping out to tinge in crimson the gray metallic bulkheads. He still always went into the room to stare at the light. Then he would sit down in the cramped chair (the ship's captain had been more like the ship's entertainer, only rarely needing to visit this room; the real commanding and piloting were accomplished by various computer algorithms). From there, Andrick would review the previous day's diagnostic reports to make sure everything was fine throughout what remained of the *Pointed Star.*

The first few days after the crash—before he was forced to develop his sanity-saving daily routine—there had been a few things to look into or repair. By profession he was a chemist, but he'd gone to graduate school on Luna, and had worked part-time to support himself at one of the moon's space junkyards, fixing up old clunkers so they could be resold. And to supplement his out-dated knowledge, the ship had videos and instructions that could walk a reasonably handy person through fixing most things.

He'd skipped meals those first few days; he'd been too busy desperately looking for other survivors, then assessing and repairing the minimal damage in the remaining part of the ship. But once all of that was done, he'd instituted a regular schedule of lunches and dinners. It was good to have a routine, though he felt that these fancy dishes, some of them with labels displaying words he couldn't pronounce, were wasted on him, who ate without enthusiasm but to sustain himself—and, later, to fill the hours too.

Because lately, only very occasionally did he have anything to look into or fix. Hyperspace ships were made well, and with several redundancies built in. They were meant to last centuries without issue —so long as their safety protocols didn't catastrophically break down.

Which, of course, they had for the *Pointed Star*. As far as Andrick could reconstruct the accident, this was what had happened: only two light years into their outboard journey, the ship's hyperspace engine had tried to fold a section of space occupied by a solid mass, likely part of the asteroid they were now permanently attached to, causing an explosion. That was never supposed to happen, of course; and in the unlikely event that it ever did, secondary protocols were supposed to kick in and move them away from the impact area at full speed. Instead, not detecting anything amiss, the ship had powered up the propulsion engine to drive right through; except, instead of the hyperspace tunnel that would have resulted from folding a cube of near-vacuum, the ship had brought them head-first into the explosion. The bubble-shaped prow had burned up and the fish-tail-shaped stern had slammed into the asteroid, the heat fusing the two objects together—saving his and Alicia's life by sealing off the hull breach.

In those project-free days, there were ten to twelve hours before he could allow himself to settle into his makeshift cot in the closet he'd turned into a bedroom, and anticipate checking the light again in the morning.

But right before the end of each day came his actual favorite part: the slow walk down the corridor, usually from the control room, to the door of the 'stern' cabin, which was now the foremost part of the surviving half of the ship. There, for only fifteen minutes, he allowed himself to watch Alicia through the clear, narrow band running down the center of the mostly frosted glass door. Having the worst cabin on the ship had saved them; everything forward had been destroyed in the crash. Their room, which Alicia had won in a virtual reality contest, was tucked away at the rear with the supplies and storage and the never-visited control room, and had survived.

He allowed himself those precious minutes of watching Alicia, tucked up in her pod, then forced himself to turn around and head to the cot he'd made from used-up supply crates.

It was a good routine, and it helped many days go by. But after eleven months, he couldn't maintain it any longer.

Marcia posed, more than relaxed, on her beach towel, her poor arms holding up her torso, one of her legs drawn up, maybe to show off her knee or ankle or something. She watched the well-muscled boys run toward and then away from the waves, while pretending she didn't notice them.

Allie smiled and let her head fall back into her hands. Marcia could waste her vacation absorbed with boys if she wanted. Allie had come here to rest; she would spend her day on this towel, doing nothing at all; dozing, maybe, warmed by the sun and cooled by the gently blowing breeze. Maybe she would let herself be convinced to take a quick—

She pulled her hands out from under her head, pushed Marcia away. Except Marcia wasn't near enough to reach. And yet Allie would've bet the rest of the vacation that Marcia had run her fingers through Allie's hair.

"Did you just touch me?" she asked.

"Weird question," Marcia said, then began humming a song.

Allie's hand shot up to her head. She'd felt it again, this time a soft hand tucking a strand of hair behind her ear.

"You okay?" Marcia said, except it wasn't Marcia. A man stooped over her; a sad-looking man with a bald head and thick eyebrows. "You okay?" Marcia's voice asked while the man's thin lips moved.

Without waiting for her response, the man reached out his hand again, stroked Allie's hair.

Allie didn't pull away from him. She felt frozen between fear at the strangeness of the situation—and an even more bewildering sense of safety. Somewhere deep down, her mind recognized that man and knew he meant her no harm.

He hummed the familiar song as he tucked her hair behind her ear. When he was finished, he leaned back and popped out of existence, instantly replaced by her friend posing on her towel, as if she'd never left.

"Marcia?"

"You okay?" Marcia asked, without looking away from the boys in the water.

Allie stood, picked up her towel, and shook the sand off the vast cosmos with its many stars and nebulae.

And then, with sudden, strange insight, as if she'd already had this realization and then forgotten it, she recognized the song: a lullaby. But had someone sung it to her as a child?

Why couldn't she remember? She pushed down the rising sense of panic, forced herself to stay calm. She couldn't remember—now that she tried—any further back than this morning, when they'd left their beach-side hotel for the short walk along the pristine sand. Then, still forcing herself to evaluate her situation calmly, she thought: pristine white sand and pristine white clouds, clear blue water and clear blue sky; a golden sun she could stare into. Shouldn't staring into the sun hurt your eyes?

Of course it should—in the real world. *You're dreaming,* she simultaneously realized and yelled at herself. *Wake up!*

When his fifteen-year old daughter won two tickets aboard the Pointed Star, Andrick Peret initially insisted that she pass on the opportunity. But, much like her mother, Alicia had a way of pushing past any resistance he offered. Also like her mother, their daughter was an eternal optimist, who saw excitement and opportunity and adventure in everything, whereas he could only see risks, dangers, obstacles.

Alicia had placed first in some virtual reality space simulation obstacle course, winning the pair of tickets aboard one of the new pleasure-cruise hyperspace ships. Previously, hyperspace had been a road traveled only by governments, large research institutions and multiplanetary corporations, but now several smaller private companies were promoting elite tourism by way of hyperspace, allowing the rich and famous to go beyond the solar system—to be one of the first human beings to visit further and further into the galaxy.

Andrick had retired the previous December. His wife, Treanne, was hip-deep working on her third major exhibit of her art, which was to open a few weeks after the Pointed Star was scheduled to return. So, if Alicia wanted to go on this trip, she needed to convince her father to accompany her.

He'd put his daughter off, but the company rep needed an answer, yes or no, so they could move ahead or move on to the next person.

"Are we even sure this is legit?" he'd tried again, that Saturday morning when casually over their weekend breakfast of pancakes and sausages, Alicia had asked if she could accept the prize.

His daughter didn't bother answering him with words; she just smiled her bright beam of optimism and nodded.

"Mmm-hmm," Andrick said. "And what about school?"

"Not to worry, father dear," she said. "We'd be a month away—total. I'll use it as my summer holidays."

"Not sure how safe it is," he mumbled.

"Hyperspace? Perfectly."

But hyperspace itself wasn't perfectly safe for human beings. Hyperspace engines, which operated by a sequential micro-folding of spacetime to traverse vast distances, had several benefits: micro-folding cost large but attainable amounts of energy and, importantly for him, time in hyperspace was non-relativistic, so people could travel those distances without their families having aged decades (or centuries) by their return. But dropping into and out of hyperspace had strange effects on the human mind: from harmless hallucinations to paranoid delusions. Which meant, these days, the explorers and adventurers and super-rich tourists visiting new stars and their systems got a nice long sleep while traveling through hyperspace, passing through the jumps in a personally-designed fantasy world rather than the haphazard daydreams and nightmares that had plagued the early adopters.

"I wouldn't even know—" He'd meant to say he didn't like virtual worlds, and would have a hard time deciding on one. But he recognized immediately what a lame excuse that was (and could imagine Alicia's thin eyebrows rising in silent, reproachful response). Instead, he stumbled on what he thought was a better excuse: "Your mom will miss us. She might need our help with the show."

Immediately he realized his mistake. Treanne, who had been watching the breakfast-table discussion with a bemused expression, had decided to stay out of it. But now he'd dragged her in.

"Mom?" Alicia said, turning to her.

"I'll be fine on the show," she said. "And of course I'll miss you both very much." He could tell from the tone of her voice what was coming next. "But I think I can survive a month."

Alicia turned her bright beam of a gaze back on him.

"Let me look into it," he said, then added ominously: "The details."

"Sure thing," Alicia said, finally digging into her breakfast.

He shot his wife a questioning glance. He hadn't expected Alicia to be put off again so easily—not without a firmer commitment from him. Treanne shrugged.

When they'd cleared the table, however, Alicia disappeared for a moment, then returned with a tablet, the contest rules already loaded on the paper-thin screen.

"Let's go over it together!" she said brightly.

He groaned, then insisted on making a second cup of tea first.

They returned to the table and she watched him eagerly as he read through the rules, taking occasional, thoughtful sips.

But every objection he uncovered, like a hopeful pig finding truffles in the earthen ground, evaporated under the glare of Alicia's unbridled enthusiasm.

Him: "There's a medical exam. You know I hate being poked and prodded."

Alicia, simply: "Yes, a free medical exam!"

Him, after reading further: "Ho, ho, look at this. 'Stern cabin!' We'll be in the smallest room, at the very butt of the ship! Next to the *engines*!"

Alicia: "We won't even know. We'll be in deep sleep! And when we get to Alpha Centauri, we'll spend most of our time in the same observation deck as everyone else."

Later—his eyes wide, and looking like a man who'd just discovered the smoking gun: "Each ticket on this thing costs as much as I made in a whole year of teaching! We'll be with a bunch of super-rich mucky-mucks!"

Alicia: "We'll make fun of them!"

A few more of his objections likewise melted under the glare of her undiminished excitement.

When he raised his head with his next semi-objection, Alicia said, staring at him fixedly, "Dad—we'll get to see Alpha Centauri's stars and planets with our own eyes. How many people can say they've done that?"

He couldn't bring himself to dash her excitement by resisting any longer.

But now, watching her in that induced semi-coma—exciting when it was a temporary part of the journey, but now as terrible as a life sentence—he wished with all of his heart that he'd been willing to break *hers*; that he had allowed the nagging, hesitant, risk-averse voice that had ruled his life until he'd met Treanne to put its oppressive foot down and squash the head of this stupid adventure.

He pushed that thought away. What was the point of driving himself crazy?

He tried not to think too much about Treanne, because doing so felt like staring at a gaping hole where his stomach should be.

Andrick mostly had great discipline. In university, after he'd drunk two full pots of coffee while staying up late to finish a paper, and made his heart beat so fast he thought he would die, he'd vowed never to have another cup. And he'd lived up to that promise.

Until he'd woken up to alarm bells, stumbling out of his pod, not fully conscious yet but registering that something bad had happened, or was happening. In a daze, he made sure Alicia was safe and still sleeping in her own pod, then he exited their room and realized that the forward half of the ship was missing, a brown wall of cold craggy rock where the door to the next corridor should've been.

Normally, a trained technician had to pull someone out of the medically-induced deep sleep that minimized cognitive side-effects when traveling through hyperspace. Then each person was shuffled to the medical room for a complete physical scan. Complications could develop from being prone for so long, even with the constant electrical stimulation provided by the sleep pod. Andrick catastrophized as a matter of course, but it wasn't strictly his own demise that concerned him. If something fatal had gone wrong deep inside his body during the long sleep, what would happen to Alicia?

He had focused on the immediate mission he'd set for himself: donning an Extravehicular Mobility Unit, or EMU, to search the asteroid on the incredibly slim chance that anyone else had survived, returning to the ship only for a little bit of sleep before fortifying himself with several cups of coffee and heading back out. It took four days to conclude what should have been evident from the beginning, that he and Alicia were the only survivors. By then, though, he'd made two discoveries: his body had survived the plunge into and climb out of induced sleep without anything worse than a few cramps and occasional muscle spasms, which soon resolved themselves. And, distracted with his work, he'd been drinking coffee without any adverse effects —so perhaps, he thought, a little bit of the poison wouldn't sting. After that, he'd allowed himself one cup each day, with breakfast.

But eleven months later, he'd lost his resolve with a different resolution: never to enter his and Alicia's cabin. He didn't know if Alicia in her induced dream state could see or hear him, but the crash alarm had jostled *him* awake, so he thought it was possible. The last thing he

wanted was for her to wake up too. Well—
the last thing he *told* himself he wanted ...
the truth was that he would've traded all
the coffee in the universe for a chance to
hear her laugh again. He couldn't do that
to her, though; in the dreamlike
simulation, she had friends (not real ones,
but she didn't know that) and a vivid
world to experience. He couldn't pull her
out of that to face reality, the rear end of a
busted spaceship her entire world and
him her only companion. Better she be in
the blissful dream-world until ... what? He
didn't know how to finish that thought.
For now he focused only on his conviction
that it was better she pass the time in the
fantasy she'd picked for herself. Better for
her to live in that dream-moment,
unaware of their predicament or of
anything beyond the fantasy world itself (a
necessary limitation of the technology,
since without the suppression of
conscious memory, the mind would reject
the dream and force the person to wake
up prematurely).

Day after day, he accepted that he
could only watch her face through the
narrow band in the glass door (the pod
covered up to her neck like a blanket, so it
could discretely both feed her body and

flush away its waste, as well as electrically stimulate muscles to prevent atrophy). Despite the translucent crown of needles on her head, she looked still and peaceful.

When his resolve to stay out finally broke, it snapped quietly. He found himself inside their cabin one day, his heart stirring at the unobstructed view of his daughter's face. Immediately, he rushed out, and kept out for days—weeks. Then one day he was inside their cabin again, but she hadn't woken or stirred, so he stayed. Then, on another day, he sat down beside her pod, out of view, reading quietly to himself. Then, later, he found himself reading out loud to her, like he had when she was an infant. Then just lightly touching her cheek with the back of his fingers, like he'd done when she'd finally fallen asleep, usually before he'd finished the story. Then he caught himself stroking her hair. Each step had emboldened him for the next.

A few days later, sitting in the part of the storeroom he called 'the cafeteria', making his small, delicious cup of coffee last as long as possible, he learned the terrible mistake he'd made. He'd been so used to near-total silence that the sound of screaming initially made him jump from the table, his heart rate sky-rocketing, looking around helplessly, furiously. Air escaping from a new breach in the hull? Then his brain sorted the echo of that sound: it had been Alicia's strained voice. He'd woken her up after all, then, called her out of her pleasant fantasy world into cold, ugly reality.

He burst into their cabin and found Alicia had pushed away the hard cover of her pod. She was sitting up, staring at the crown of needles in her hand, angry red cat's claw scratch marks on her forehead from where she'd ripped off the device.

"I couldn't get it off," she croaked, her long-unused vocal chords still straining under the effort to speak. "I started panicking."

"It's off now," he said, gently.

A faltering smile finally broke through. "I'm okay, Dad. I'm okay. It was ... not what I thought it would be like." Her voice still sounded strange and pained, but her regular cadence, the rapid cascade of words, was returning. "And they really need to work on the whole waking-up part. That was *not* pleasant." Finally she noticed something in his expression. "Dad?"

"In a minute, darling," he said. "Get out of that pod and get dressed, but wait for me here. I'll get you a glass of water. Are you hungry?"

She shook her head. "What's going on?"

"Okay. Just water. Wait for me here."

He hurried out of the room before she could stop him. He needed time to think, to organize his words.

But when he returned holding the unsealed bottle of water, he still didn't know what to say. Alicia had gotten dressed, and had brushed her hair, and now sat waiting for him on the edge of the pod, which she'd converted into a regular bed.

"Something bad happened," she said, accepting the bottle.

He sat beside her and, staring ahead, told her about waking up to the alarm, determining that everyone else had perished in the crash, setting up the distress signal ... which had gone unanswered for almost a year now. "I'm sorry, honey," he finished, finally turning to look at her.

Her face had paled. He indicated the water, and she forced the bottle up to her lips and took the smallest sip before bringing it down again and saying, "Dad—it's not your fault."

"I'm sorry about waking you up. I did, didn't I?"

"I started seeing you in my dream. Hearing your voice. But I didn't know it was you. You touched my hair?"

"I convinced myself it wouldn't wake you."

She hopped off the bed, suddenly energized, the water sloshing in the bottle and some spilling onto the ground. "You should've woken me up right away!" Alicia wiped up the spilled water with the toes of her socks. "I could've helped you."

Andrick stared at the bulkhead where it met the overhead. "At first I wanted to know what the situation was. I wanted to make sure we were safe. Then I set up the distress beacon and I thought I should let you sleep until we got rescued. I didn't want to wake you up to this—"

"And if we didn't get rescued? You would've let me sleep forever? Until I died? Or you died?"

He didn't answer. But he didn't need to. He'd spent the last year so terrified he'd accidentally force her to leave the comfort of her dream world that he'd never imagined Alicia would be upset with him for *not* waking her up.

She paced the small room, marching up and down its length as if a sentry on duty. He had the same tic; he needed to move his body to work his brain.

"How about some breakfast?" he ventured after watching her cross the room a half-dozen times.

She stopped short. "I have questions. Honest answers only!"

"Okay," he said.

"Is there enough food and water?"

"The storeroom wasn't harmed. We won't starve, even if we live to be a hundred each."

"Oxygen, energy, heat—things like that. How long before we run out?"

"You don't have to worry about that. The engines, the batteries, life support .. none of that was harmed. That isn't the issue."

"What's the issue?"

"It's just you and me, darling." He studied the bulkhead again, no longer able to meet his daughter's judgmental, still-angry stare. "That's it. For the rest of our lives."

"You said the engines are fine," she said, as if only then processing the words. "Can't we just—"

"Fly away?" He fought back a smile. "We lost half our ship ... more than half ... but we gained an asteroid thirty times its original size. The propulsion system can't handle that kind of mass."

"Can we cut ourselves free?"

The thought hadn't occurred to him, but he knew instantly it wouldn't work. They had access to hand-held welding torches, but they were very low-powered ... he and his daughter could spend an entire day out there and only lightly scratch the surface of the asteroid. "It would take a long time," he said. "Longer than we have." With a grunt, he pushed himself onto his feet. "We have the distress signal," he said, trying to inject into his voice a note of optimism that he didn't feel. "Our best bet is to wait for rescue."

"Our best bet is the signal that's gone unanswered for a year?"

He couldn't look at her. Yesterday, the thought that he'd be standing here having a conversation with his daughter would have filled him with joy, but now, in actuality, he was faced with his own failure—to get them out of this mess, yes, but also to keep her blissfully asleep so she wouldn't have to face the stark reality of their doomed lives.

He almost jumped at a touch; she had placed her hand on his arm. Before he could turn toward her, she pulled him into a tight embrace. Because her head reached only to his chest, and she spoke into it, he almost missed the words, but not the tone. Hadn't she been furious with him? Didn't she realize the severity—the hopelessness—of their situation? But, gently, she had said, "And that's why you need me."

"What?" he said, pulling her away from him.

"Dad!" *Oh, my wonderful dumb-dumb dad*, her tone said, that familiar, wonderful enthusiasm. "Are you kidding? There's *much* more we can do!"

If Alicia had slept for the next year ... or five, or ten, or a hundred, he didn't doubt that he would've kept on checking his distress signal every day. What else was there to do?

Well—Alicia had plenty of ideas.

He tried, over the next few days, to entertain her with games or movies or books (he'd screened them for her, he said; played or watched or read them all in advance during the long daytime hours, so he could point her toward the best ones) but his daughter only wanted to debate ideas. And, if he failed to convince her that one wouldn't work, they had to try it right away: silly things like literally carving 'SOS' in large letters into all sides of their potato-shaped asteroid (which took them three weeks in EMUs with the welding torches) to more serious endeavors like erecting a series of mirrors and debris painted with reflective paint to send their distress signal in many more directions.

He always poked around for holes in her ideas. Her job was to bring up wacky notions and his to knock them down, he told her. If he won, they took that day off and read books and watched movies, and if she won, they spent however long it would take to make her idea a reality, which usually meant putting on the many pieces of their EMU suits and trekking into the cold, ever-present night of space on the asteroid Alicia had named Potato Island.

She was so enthusiastic that it took him a long time—too long—to notice that something was wrong.

When Alicia was very young, probably five or six, she'd cut herself while playing in their living room. It was only when he saw drops of blood all over the floor that she showed him the deep gash across her thumb. A toy had fallen into the floor vent; she'd removed the register and fished around for her little figurine, slicing open her thumb in the process. But she hadn't wanted to stop playing, she said. Alicia's soaring optimism had its dark side; she could set aside concerns with terrible ease, assuming things would work themselves out.

Now she had hidden for weeks what he suspected was a blood clot that had formed in her left calf. She had begun to limp, and when he asked about it, she said her leg hurt a little. By the time he examined her, her calf had swelled up to twice the size of the other, the skin had turned red and very hot to the touch, and she screamed out in pain when he squeezed the muscle gently.

"Oh, darling," he said.

"It'll be fine," she said, shooing him away, jumping off her bed, but unable to stop herself from wincing. "Okay, so it hurts a lot, but it's far from my heart, right?"

The scanning equipment that could've confirmed the clot had burned up with the rest of the medical room; so had the medicines, like blood thinners, that could've helped.

"Any trouble breathing?" he said, looking up from the tablet.

"None!" she said, sucking back a deep lungful.

He didn't tell her what he'd just read: a warning about pulmonary embolism, which would happen if the clot dislodged and traveled up to the lungs. He doubted Alicia would give it much thought anyway, even though it was a fatal condition; she'd dismiss the possibility as an outside chance and get on with her life.

From then on, though, every cough, every clearing of the throat, made him whip his head around to stare at her. She finally told him he was making her feel like a time bomb he expected to go off, and she wanted him to stop. But her limp got worse.

And if she did develop an embolism? What could he do, without equipment, training, supplies?

The specific fear of something happening to Alicia before they could be rescued focused his mind, forced it into considering ideas he would've dismissed as reckless, fueled by the real pain he saw escaping onto the grimaces on her face whenever she walked and by the ever-present shadow of something even more serious pursuing her.

When it finally came to him in the middle of one sleepless night, the solution arrived with a freezing chill of recognition: yes, this was their best chance to get home quickly; and yes, this could be the last thing they tried, and in that case there'd be nothing recognizable left for any ship that did eventually find their wreckage. But sometimes, he told himself, ideas seem brilliant to a sleepy mind, and lose their luster in daylight. He half-hoped that would be the case, and went back to sleep.

He woke to the sounds of weeping. Alicia was sitting up in bed, left leg pulled up, gripping her calf as if desperately trying to hold off the pain with her hands.

"How bad?" he said, sitting up.

She shook her head but couldn't speak for a minute.

"There's something we can try," he said, speaking through a sudden constriction in his throat, "to get home."

"Let's hear it," she croaked, then stretched out her leg again and turned to face him.

He hesitated. "It's incredibly dangerous, actually. Really desperate. And even if it works, probably futile."

"Dad, spit it out."

He spat it out: "We fold the space just beyond Potato Island. Touching it only a little."

"But that would … cause an explosion."

"It would. A small one. But perhaps enough to propel us back toward Luna. We could, maybe, correct our direction by folding space at angles to Potato Island."

She'd been listening intently. "Okay, let's try it!" she said suddenly, excitement or hope, perhaps, chasing away the pain from her mind for a moment. He was glad for that, anyway.

"Let me lay out my concerns, okay?"

"I'm sold already," she said, shrugging playfully. "Why risk changing my mind?"

"Just listen. The hyperspace drive has safety protocols to make sure it doesn't send out a beam to fold space occupied by a significant mass. But I've spent a lot of time studying the ship and what went wrong, and I think the malfunction that caused us to crash into the asteroid will also allow us to blow up pieces of Potato Island."

"Great!"

"Not really. The protocols are there for a reason. There's a risk—a big one—that we'll miscalculate and blow ourselves up. Or cause another breach. Or—"

"Yes, yes. But how will we know unless we try?"

"Very funny."

"Two light years, Dad," she said, more seriously. "We can't let that small of a distance keep us from mom."

"Two light years is not ..." He let the thought trail off as unnecessary to complete.

"Hold on, what's the rest of your idea? Just pushing ourselves toward Sol doesn't get us very far very fast, does it? It would take thousands of years..."

He waited for her to figure out.

"Ah!" she said, after a moment. "We carve away enough of Potato Island ..."

"Yes," he said.

"... then we fold space properly and go through under propulsion! And *boom*, we're home."

"Well, hopefully not *boom*."

Alicia stepped onto the floor gingerly, testing her weight before trusting her leg, and hobbled over to sit beside him. "I know there are significant risks. But we should try. They would've found us by now. You're right: two light years is an immense distance. But if that's all that's keeping us from mom? Don't you think we *have* to try?"

"Okay," he said. "We'll try. Carefully!"

Carefully meant that Andrick first wanted to test the beam on cubes of empty space far away from them; when he'd satisfied himself, they tried folding the space barely touching the edge of Potato Island. He was right about the ship's malfunction; it didn't even give a warning. And once it was done, they hardly felt the explosion—if there was one.

"Closer," Alicia said.

Again there was no warning, but this time they felt the explosion as a small rumble under their feet. And if nothing else, Potato Island was now moving in a direction more toward Sol than it had been before.

"Again," Alicia said, clapping her hands.

Fold by fold, Alicia tried to push him to blow up larger and larger chunks of Potato Island. But having found a distance from the Island he felt reasonably comfortable with, Andrick insisted they maintain discipline.

Day after day they carved away chunks of the asteroid, Andrick working until he collapsed, Alicia unsuccessfully hiding how much her calf hurt most of the time. It took almost a month before they felt they had sliced off enough mass to try moving under propulsion. So far, after weeks of work, they'd barely moved any closer to Sol, of course. But with both drives running? They could be home in a few days.

"Ready?" he said. They sat in the storeroom, Andrick holding the tablet he used to manipulate the software that was designed, ninety-nine times out of a hundred, to control itself.

"Do it," Alicia said, sitting across from him.

He took a deep breath, then shook his head and slid the tablet across the table. "You do the honors."

She glanced down at the screen, then—without any ceremony—stabbed the bright square button with her finger.

The propulsion drive sprang to life, humming its soft song throughout the ship's decks, beginning to move them through space even with the remaining mass of Potato Island attached.

"It worked?" Andrick said, hardly able to believe it.

Alicia twirled around and around in the chair, though if circumstances were different, he knew, she'd be on her feet, dancing, leaping around, laughing madly.

As he watched her, he felt the wide smile on his face crumble away. Because now he had to face the reality of their situation: yes, they could create a wave of micro-folds, from here to Luna, and drive their ship through them. They could be entering Sol within the week. But who would they be when they arrived? Hyperspace had strange and ugly effects on the conscious human mind. And … something was wrong with this hyperspace drive. Something that was beyond his abilities to uncover, let alone fix: the error in mass-detection that had caused the crash in the first place and that had allowed them to carve away most of Potato Island.

"We have to risk it," Alicia said, when she'd stopped twirling long enough to ask him what was wrong.

"No."

She sat back down. "We didn't do all—"

"We're no good to anyone—no good to your mom—if we show up having lost our minds."

"But dad—"

"We'll have to drop down to one fold a day. I'd rather travel while we're awake and can guarantee the space is empty, but the risk is too high. Instead we'll identify the area we're going to fold in the evening, then set the commands to activate in the middle of the night so that the ship goes through folded space while we're sleeping. You can add to your bedtime prayers that nothing enters the area we've identified in the hours between setting and activating the engine. But we have to tolerate some level of risk," he continued, and had enough self-awareness to know that he was speaking now, not to Alicia, but to the risk-averse part of himself, "and I think that one is pretty low. We'll try it tonight and monitor for effects. Okay?"

She bit her lower lip, then said, "Okay."

That night, they instructed the ship to create a micro-fold at two in the morning and drive through it. Andrick had a terrible time falling asleep, and considered deleting the instructions; but from her snoring, Alicia didn't have similar trouble and he tried to put the worries out of his mind ... and then it was morning. He turned over quickly and picked up the tablet.

Alicia stirred as he studied the star charts. "Did it work?" she said, sitting up.

He nodded, then met her eyes. "How do you feel?"

"Oh, fine. I'm fighting to suppress this weird homicidal urge to strangle you, but otherwise I feel totally sane."

"Very funny."

The following day they instructed the ship to repeat the process.

They didn't feel any adverse effects then either, or after any of the other nights.

"We're on our way home, darling," Andrick said to Alicia.

Their joy was genuine but muted. If they stuck to their single fold-and-travel per night, it would take almost a decade to get home. Even if they risked two or three fold-and-travel cycles during the night—a huge risk, given the drive's inability to properly detect and avoid massive objects—it would still take years. As for traveling through a fold while they were awake, so they could fold and monitor for objects, fold and monitor for objects … Andrick had heard too many horror stories about what the early hyperspace travelers experienced to allow himself to contemplate that option except as a last, desperate resort.

It turned out that wouldn't be necessary. When rescue came, though, it almost killed them all.

Because of all of their jumping around, beaming out distress calls from different points in space, one of those signals had finally been picked up by an outpost station in orbit around Pluto. A search and rescue ship called the *Corner Lights* was immediately dispatched.

Loud banging woke Andrick up just as he'd fallen asleep. For a moment he thought he'd imagined the sound, but Alicia had woken up too, startled, and then they heard again the urgent *thud-thud-thud*.

Something's gone wrong with the engine, Andrick thought in panic, and stumbled out of bed desperately to see if he could shut it down before it exploded. But in the passageway the *thud-thud-thud* banged again.

Through the airlock portholes, he saw what he'd dreamed of one day seeing: friendly human faces waving at him, though he was surprised they wore no helmets or EMUs. Was he still asleep, dreaming of this rescue by people who could float in space and breathe vacuum? But then he saw the structure extending behind them and realized that they'd established a pressurized tunnel between the two ships.

As good-naturedly as he could, Andrick waved off the hugging and celebrating to ask if they had a medic on board, and on being told of course they did, to beg that they look at Alicia's leg right away. In the meantime, his daughter had hobbled out to see what was happening, so they picked her up and whisked her through the tunnel and into the *Corner Lights*, Andrick racing to keep up, and into their medical room. There the doctor, an old woman with a brusque manner, shooed them away after they'd put Alicia down on the hospital bed, but grudgingly allowed Andrick to stay. "Very bad," she said, after a few minutes examining Alicia, shaking her head. "You should go," she said, "your daughter is in good hands."

"Very bad?" Andrick repeated in a whisper.

The old woman pushed him out the door with remarkable strength. "Could be worse," she said, in that oblivious, matter-of-fact way some doctors had. "Probably would've killed her within a few weeks. But she'll be fine now. Routine surgery, a few hours of rest, and she'll be jumping around like nothing ever happened."

Somewhat dazed, Andrick allowed someone to lead him back to the mess, where he was sat down at a table and handed a hot cup of coffee by a young officer named Cedric, who'd clearly been assigned as his minder.

"We'll have to wait for the doctor's all-clear," Cedric said. "Then we'll get everyone back into deep sleep and get you home. Before we dismantle the tunnel to the Pointed Star, is there anything we can bring back for you? We've collected the personal effects you had in your cabin."

Andrick shook his head; he couldn't think of a single souvenir he wanted of that experience, thank you very much. "Can I record a message for my wife?" he said.

The young man nodded and said, with evident pride, "The *Corner Lights* has hyperspace bottles."

Well, Andrick thought, *we sure could've used hyperspace message-in-a-bottle probes on the* Pointed Star. He began to voice the thought, but his throat had suddenly gone dry.

Cedric had stood and was waiting for Andrick to follow him, but Andrick's legs had lost their strength. He forced his arm up to eye-level and checked his wrist. In under twenty minutes, the hyperspace engine on the Pointed Star would try to fold space, with no safeguards to stop it in case any part of the *Corner Lights* touched its folding field.

"I need to get back to the ship," he said, turning wild eyes on his minder, adrenaline finally unlocking his body so that he nearly toppled over the table when he jumped to his feet. "Now!"

To his credit, Cedric didn't hesitate. He nodded once, then sprinted down corridors until they reached the tunnel, where he stepped aside for Andrick to lead the way.

The race to the cabin was a blur he could never quite remember. Some memory of stumbling down the semi-rigid material of the tunnel, shoving open the airlock doors, launching himself into the cabin to grab the tablet and delete the instructions, Cedric on his heels the whole time, asking something that didn't register at the time.

"It's okay," he said, collapsing into the chair to allow his pulse to resettle.

"You're sure?" Cedric said, breathing heavily himself.

Andrick closed his eyes and nodded.

"All right. I'll let you be then. You know your way back when you're ready to join us?"

Andrick nodded again without opening his eyes.

After a few minutes, his breath and heart-rate under control, he stood again. If anyone on that poor rescue ship had known how close they'd come to, at best, a very unnecessary and stupid risk... He shook off the feeling and began heading to the tunnel, when he stopped and looked back. The light he'd wired to their SOS signal was no longer blinking red, of course. How many countless hours had he stared at that tiny light, praying for it to blink green, just once? Now it was blinking green continuously and he'd almost left without noticing.

Now that would be a souvenir, wouldn't it?

The risk-averse Andrick warned him against tampering any further with the ship. No doubt there would be an investigation—at the very least, they'd want to know what had gone wrong with the hyperspace engine—and he didn't need to explain to anyone why he'd felt the need to help himself to a part of their ship.

Oh, do shut up, he told himself. He unscrewed the cover from the dashboard, removed the small light, and stuck it into his pocket. Satisfied, he left the cabin without looking back and climbed into the tunnel, closing the airlock doors behind him.

Back aboard the *Corner Lights*, Andrick sent Treanne a message and, in the time he waited to be allowed to see Alicia again, even received one in response. He could hardly understand his wife because she kept crying, almost hyperventilating, through her words. But he understood her intent and sent her one more message to say that he loved her too and they both couldn't wait to see her again—very soon now.

When the doctor finally let him into the medical room, Alicia was sitting up in the recovery bed and looking better than she had in months. He thought he'd known how much the pain from her calf had caused her, but only now, seeing the contrast in her relaxed face and easy smile, did he realize the extent of her previous suffering.

"Hello, my face in the clouds," she said, tucking her legs to the side to make room for him. "Why so glum?"

"Face in the clouds?" he said, sitting down beside her.

She only broadened her smile at his confusion, then cupped the side of his face with her palm. She'd done that even as a toddler, reaching out whenever she thought he was upset. "Aren't we going home now, Dad?"

"Yes, darling. We are."

"Good," she said. "You see? Everything worked out. And don't worry, next time I win tickets aboard a hyperspace ship, our trip will go *much* smoother."

In the past he'd never been able to help but rise to Alicia's bait. This time, however, he just shook his head, said, "Sure it will, darling," then laughed and pulled his daughter into a tight embrace.

See Karl El-Koura's story "Anamnesis" online at Metaphorosis.
If you liked it, leave a comment. Authors love that!
Remember to subscribe to our e-mail updates so you'll know when new stories are posted.

About the story

I once read every word of Philip K. Dick's *Exegesis* (that might not sound like much of an accomplishment, unless you're familiar with that door-stopper of a book). I believe that's where I picked up the word that forms the title of the story, which means a forgetting of forgetting, or a remembering again.

Seemingly separately, as I watched my young daughter grow, I knew that there would come a time when she'd ask me questions that would leave me with two choices: speak the truth as I saw it (in an age-appropriate way, of course) or tell her a lie that would comfort her, or help her fit in, or keep her out of trouble.

Then one day I had a mental image, 'as if some cosmic god had stuck his nose into the mist, which had molded around his face'.

The three experiences melded together to form the genesis for "Anamnesis". The story is in part my answer to the question of where I should land when answering my daughter's questions. Reality is better than illusion, it seems to me, even if it can be more uncomfortable.

A question for the author

Q: What would your characters say about you?

A: I fear they would say: "Clean your ears, bud. What I said was much more interesting than what you wrote down." I hope they would say: "Thanks for letting us find our own way." I expect they would say: "Well—you did your best."

About the author

Karl El-Koura lives with his family in Canada's capital city, holds a second-degree black belt in Okinawan Goju Ryu karate, and works a regular job in daylight while writing fiction at night. "Anamnesis" is his third appearance in Metaphorosis. His stories "The Azurian Shield" and "Her Last Will" were published in the October 2021 and September 2022 issues, respectively.

www.ootersplace.com, @KarlElKoura

The Zoo Diaries V

Frances Pauli

Part Five

Previously…

At the Rainriver Zoological Gardens, one escape became the catalyst for a series of unfortunate incidents. The tortoise, Oliver, roamed the zoo as a fugitive, searching for his missing cage mate, Miranda. His adventure has taken him to the Aviary, where he was recaptured only to dig free again, this time with the help of the duplicitous crow, who led him to the Marshland and helped him slip under the net.

While the zoo's photography contest set the crowds wild, their poor behavior heaped extra stress upon the already troubled animals. The spike in attendance boded well for the bottom line, but the zoo was forced to hire armed security to keep the mobs in line.

While the other animals dealt with the increased interaction, Oliver searched the Marshland for his lost love, unaware that the crows were watching and that his reunion was not likely to go as planned.

CONTEST

When the contest results are tallied, zoo management calls an emergency meeting. The victor is problematic, but it has won by a landslide. 'Lion Eats Cellphone' has blown away all competition, but the repercussions have caused nothing but difficulties.

Security reports a need for more boots on the ground. Janitorial gives a presentation in which they display 25 glossy photos of trash and detritus littering every corner of the zoo, including a shot of the interior lion paddock with each foreign item circled in red ink.

The lead veterinarian speaks for ten minutes on the dangers of ingested plastic on a lion's digestive track. During his speech, the head of marketing is caught nodding off.

Someone's nephew suggests altering the results online.

The deception is given serious consideration, but marketing believes it would cause a PR nightmare.

In the end it is decided. 'Lion Eats Cellphone' will be disqualified for violation of zoo regulations. The video owner will receive half the cash award but no mention other than a reiteration of zoo policy and a public post on the safety of zoo animals and property.

The official winner is now 'Avian Courtship'. A distant second place is another Charlie video, 'Lion Licks Little Boy'.

Everyone is satisfied except the owner of 'Lion Eats Cellphone', who takes the cash but continues to insist it was an accidental drop. The internet discusses the event with some heat, a great deal of insults and over-explaining, and complaints on all sides.

Eventually, the contest is forgotten. The zoo webpage visitor count returns to its pre-popularity state, and someone's nephew finds a summer job working at the local burger joint. Zoo attendance is still up, and the website never mentions the second tortoise escape.

The keeper team reports evidence of stress on their animals. Increased traffic, they believe, is beginning to affect the behavior of their charges. They are listened to briefly and then assured that the contest's end will reduce attendance.

It is only temporary.

Things will settle down soon, and in the meantime, the money might be used to improve conditions.

Or to expand the gift shop.

The employee appreciation potluck is pitched as a reward for the staff's perseverance. Signup sheets fill quickly with offers to bring pie, potato salad, and lots and lots of hot dogs.

Hyena Pen

Alice falls asleep in the cat house, curled into a blanket that no longer smells odd. She has been twitching all day today, growing warm and uncomfortable. And very lonely. She awakens back in her own cage.

The floor is smooth and littered with straw. The stair-step rock stands guard from the corner. Her water basin is exactly where she remembers it belongs, but everything smells different. Only the blanket beneath her suggests it is not a hostile scent, that this, too, should have been expected.

Alice lifts her square head, opens her mouth, and cackles out her nerves. From the uppermost stair-step another hyena answers with a low growl.

She is not threatened by this. His scent may be all over her cage, but it is familiar, hers now as much as the rock is.

He only needs to be taught.

She stands, bracing all four legs in a stiff, bristling pose. Her ears move non-stop, and she takes a few jerking steps toward the water. Her mouth is fuzzy, and she will be able to see the intruder more easily from across the cage.

He growls again but there is no force behind it, no authority.

Alice ignores him but drinks with her ears aimed, always, in his direction. He shifts atop the rock. He sniffs and rumbles, but he is smart enough not to surrender the perch.

He has her at a disadvantage, however, in position only. Alice knows this, as she knows every inch of the stair-step surface. She waits, letting her tail flick and her ears swivel. She rises and pees, moving around the cage as she does to spread the urine. She covers his stink with her own mark and is thrilled when he growls again.

Alice waits. She knows many tricks. He will want to sniff and circle. He will need to come down soon enough.

She gives him her back, stares through the bars and pretends to watch the pathways. It is light already. The zoo will open soon. Alice hears him slip to the second tier and smiles.

Her body is still, relaxed, and non-threatening. Her mind is sharp. He reaches the third step where she could easily leap at him. Alice lies down.

The other hyena slinks to the floor. He moves, not to her directly, but to the blanket instead. He buries his nose in it, smells his own odor overlain with hers.

Always on top.

Alice waits until he moves to the corner, until he begins to follow the trail of her urine.

"This cage is mine," she says without looking at him. "You don't belong here."

His voice is deep and jagged. There is something about it, however, that she likes. "I am here," he says simply.

Alice sits, yawns, and listens to the padding of his feet. His breath is heavy as he drinks her in, his steps too soft, too confident. When she lunges, he is off guard, distracted, and foolish.

Alice hits him in the side with her full weight. He rolls under the impact, and she is on him, pinning his spotted body to the ground and holding his delicate throat in her heavy jaws. His body is rigid, fights her for three long breaths. Then, as easily as a sigh, he softens. He relaxes beneath her, and she has won.

There was never any doubt of this.

Alice releases him and sits. He rolls onto his belly, groveling, whimpering, and trying to lick her muzzle without lifting too high and earning another reprimand.

"You are mine," Alice says, and he wriggles and sinks lower. "Everything is mine."

"Yes."

She thinks she likes the sound of him even more now. His smell is not foul, and she has itched for company for many days.

"Who are you?" Alice asks.

"I am Rocko," he answers, cringing when she growls. He corrects his mistake quickly. "I am yours."

"Yes," Alice says.

She allows him to rub against her chin, to whine and scoot in homage before she leaps away, bounding to the apex of the stair-step rock to wait for him.

Ape House

Gonzo's elation carries him to the highest ropes. He has found his bean again. Five black cherries waited for him on the ledge this morning. Five perfect crunchy bites that stop his shaking and bring his headache fast to bay.

He chewed four of these immediately, his excitement too much to resist, his need too powerful. Today, however, he has managed to reserve the' fifth. He means to savor it.

Gonzo hides it in one clenched fist and hoots down at a troop that seems sluggish today. The other macaques pass through the square door one by one, blinking into the sunlight and reaching for the lower vines with empty paws and full bellies. Gonzo has forgotten to eat.

He peels back his lips and screeches at them. He hoots, and his fangs flash. They are stained today, marked by the bean juice and ready to display that color proudly.

The others show him halfhearted smiles, pale teeth in slow mouths. He thinks they'll try to steal his bean, and he stuffs the last cherry into his mouth, chews with his lips sealed while the juices drain down his throat.

The cage vibrates around him. The world slows and Gonzo imagines he is king over all of it. His bean is speed and power, and with it between his teeth, he believes he can reach out to the whole zoo, grip it all in a tight paw, and crush it slowly between his leathery fingers.

Wolf Run

Raksha is named after a famous wolf mother, but she does not know it. She is not likely to ever encounter a book. She *is* a wolf, *and* a mother, however, and like her literary counterpart, she is made of patience.

Today, her pups are sulking. They have been less active, choosing to lie in a place even when the sunlight has moved past them. She fears for their bellies, fears the worms that sometimes kill a pup's drive to grow and to thrive.

Raksha calls them to her, and they drag their tiny bodies across the grass. The female sits, but the male pup flops onto his side, tongue lolling. His belly looks full but healthy enough, neither distended nor sparse of fur.

"Are you ill, my pups?" Raksha asks.

Their 'no's echo one another, flat and listless.

"But something had taken the pounce out of you," Raksha insists. "You must tell me."

The pups exchange a look that hangs from them like a weight. The male covers his nose with both paws. His sister answers for them both.

"We want freedom," she says, sitting taller and flattening her ears to her head. "We want to go beyond the high wall."

Raksha lets slip a low growl. Her ears lay tight to her skull, and she sits back on her haunches. This is not at all what she expected. Far worse than a belly full of parasites.

Their minds have been poisoned.

"Who told you about freedom?" she asks.

"A pigeon told us." The pup's answer is heartsick, twangs with longing for the unknown.

"Pigeons are liars," Raksha tries, though she can see the light in the pups' eyes. She can see the damage that has already been done. "What does a pigeon know of anything?"

"She flew away," the male pup answers. "She went over the wall."

"And might easily be dead now," Raksha says. "Might be eaten or ravaged."

"Do you think so?" There is interest in the female pup's voice. There is more energy than Raksha has seen from her in days.

"I do." She latches on to the opening. "Birds are too stupid to know anything. They are not *wolves*."

"And freedom?"

The girl pup leans into her question. Her brother's ears lift from his skull. Their eyes drill into their mother.

They are practically begging for the lie.

"What do you like best about being a wolf?" Raksha asks.

"Sitting on the tallest rock," the girl pup barks it, sure of herself.

Her brother mumbles, "Eating the fat bugs that live under our log."

"Then do that," Raksha proclaims. "Do that as often as you possibly can."

"What do bugs and rocks have to do with—"

Raksha cuts off the pup's argument with a growl. "It makes you happy," she says. "Do the thing that makes you happy. *That* is freedom, my cubs."

"Are you sure?" The male pup whines, but his tail thumps against the grass.

"I am quite sure," Raksha says. "You must do what makes you happy."

She watches them carefully, and even though she has won, they seem much older when they answer.

"Yes, Mother."

Grizzly Caged

Hector's box is rolled on eight metal casters down the long hallway. She-who-takes-notes is there, along with his other doctors. When he poses and presses his paw for them, they offer a skewer of grapes through the bars.

She-who-takes-notes does not clap, but her smile soothes him.

The end of his box is positioned against a dark wall with much jostling and mutters from the doctors' servants. There are more bars along that surface, but they slide aside. Someone grumbles in the dim light while Hector chews his treats.

Metal screeches. A square of light appears, drawing his gaze down. When he can look without blinking, he is surprised to see the interior of his own den. The box has been wedged against it, and with a click and the effort of many human paws, the end slides upward.

Hector is free to go home.

He stuffs the grapes between his black lips and looks at She-who-takes-notes. The den smells of him. Beyond it, he can see a sliver of his fallen log. He has been content in the box with the grapes and the doctors, but his artist is out there.

She is probably worried about him.

Hector groans despite the fact that he is pain-free. He ambles slowly from the cage, crosses his den, and sits while the bars move again. For a single moment, he can see the doctors through them. Then the wall comes down, and it is as if they never were.

Hector moves easily. His body has mended. He feels, in fact, stronger than he has in decades, younger and fiercer.

At his railing, the sun tells him he is late. The artist has missed him today, has come and gone already.

Hector is sorry to disappoint her, but there is always tomorrow. He will be ready by then. He will show her just how much of a bear he can be.

He lopes from his den like a cub would run. His joints make no comment, and Hector lifts onto his hind legs. He stretches toward the sun, poses, and shows the clicking cameras at the railing all his teeth.

He is bear.

Tomorrow, he will be ready to shine.

Elephant Paddock

Shanti has stopped counting. Today she draws pictures with her straw. She piles it into tortoise-shaped sculptures or flattens smooth canvases of yellow gold and then removes bits to expose an Oliver-shaped portrait in the negative spaces.

Occasionally, she mutters. "One tortoise," but through most of her work, she is concentrating far too hard to worry about how many pieces of straw it takes to build a tortoise shell. How many swipes of her trunk equal a suitable likeness?

She is inspired, obsessed. She has found her muse, and he is shaped like a stone and covered in perfect, patterned, hexagons.

Lion Enclosure

Charlie chews in his sleep now. His tawny jaws work around his pink tongue, masticating the memory of squeaky meat, of morsels offered by the crowd to their maned god. He lies in the sun, sprawled on his side with his mouth partway open. His tail twitches as he chews nothing.

His dream veldt is populated by hotdog gazelles. Great herds of migrating beasts with sausage legs and long tube necks. They squeak when they walk, filling the Savannah with their delicious cries. Filling Charlie's head and making him salivate freely.

The air is a thick blanket of scent, of rich sweet meat and spicy preservatives.

It is driving him mad.

He dreams the lionesses hunt for him, but they are far afield, dark shadows on the horizon only. Charlie chews the scent. He swallows the idea of the meat, tasting from memory. He is obsessed. The squeaking meat has possessed him.

His tongue lolls against dry grass. His teeth rise and fall, and deep in his long gut, a desperate rumble echoes like a mighty roar.

The Crow

Debra circles the marshland three times to make certain she has enough time. The tortoise moves like a slug, one lumbering foot at a time. Even ecstatic, he is mud flowing, weighted down by his ponderous nature.

He is pointed in the right direction, but Debra is sure he will not reach his goal before she returns.

She must not miss that moment, but her victory will be sweeter with an audience. She needs the murder to witness it, needs the other crows to appreciate exactly what she has done.

She circles again, marks Oliver's progress, and then angles away. The zoo blurs below as she cries out to her fellow crows.

At the old bear's cage, she gathers a pair of birds who have already grown bored waiting for him to be injured again. A low sweep over the cat house brings three more. As she flies, Debra calls to her kin. She screeches a promise of sport that is far greater than their ordinary games.

The murder responds with a collective cackle. They gather around Debra, adding their wings, their voices, to her cause.

"Come," the croaking voices sing. "Come, come and see."

By the time the murder returns to the marshland, it is as if a black cloud descends upon the nets.

Tortoise Abroad

Oliver calls Miranda's name as he trundles through the marshland. His steps churn, as much as a tortoise is capable of churning, and he drags his shell past a low duck pond where teals and loons mingle their regal shapes with those of the common mallard.

He sticks to the paths, and once he reaches that solid firmament, progresses quickly. The fences here, like those in the farm, are wooden and open enough for tortoises to pass below the bottom rail. A few have wire behind them, however, and he sees with a sinking heart that this is usually where the long-legged birds are found.

He passes storks and flamingos, egrets with frilled heads and cranes that stalk to the front of their enclosures to gawk at him as he passes.

Oliver asks them all about his heron, and they all give the same answer.

"Move along."

"Just down a few more."

Oliver thanks them, but his elation is fading. He thinks he will never reach her, thinks the universe is adding cages between them so that each time he passes one, three more spawn further down the line.

His steps begin to stutter. He pulls his head halfway into his shell and stamps onward. At each fence he cries Miranda's name, and he almost fails to notice when the birds beyond the fence begin to look like her.

Oliver steps and pivots. There is a wooden fence, but he ignores it. His legs carry him easily underneath, across the strip of mowed grass to the short wire wall inside. It is not unlike the one around his own home.

Beyond it, five long-legged, tan-bodied, curl-necked herons stand. They cluster in the rear of their pen, where the grass grows long, and a high arc of reeds marks some pond or other waterway.

"Miranda." The first time it comes out as a whisper. Oliver stretches his neck, tries to see his love in the huddle of so-similar birds. "Miranda!"

She looks his way. He sees her graceful neck stretch and twist. He holds his breath as she detaches herself from the flock. His eyes tear.

Miranda moves toward him with all the elegance he remembers. She glides on her stilt legs, and her downy neck is an ess holding her wedge-shaped head aloft.

"Oliver?" Her voice is a nutshell cracking. "What are you doing here?"

He doesn't notice it at first, the way she turns to look over her shoulder, the way she lowers, bending and flexing her legs so that she is a screen between the flock and his domed body. Until she unfurls one wing to hide him, Oliver misses the cool note in her words. The sharp glint in the eye aimed in his direction.

"I— I came to find you," he says.

"You escaped?" Only in that he hears a speck of interest.

"I did," he agrees with too much vehemence.

Miranda takes a step away. "You'll be punished."

"I didn't know where you were," he blurts, sensing her drawing away, understanding only on the surface what has to come next. "You were just gone."

"They moved me here," Miranda's tone veers again, sounding at last as he remembers it. Bright and haughtily, she informs him, "They were building us a new enclosure, you see, a space with room for all of these *new* herons."

"New herons," Oliver parrots.

"Oh, yes. Fresh in, all of them. The two females are from another zoo, as is Manuel. But my mate, Evan, was caught *in the wild.*"

"Evan." Oliver's neck lowers, slips back inside his shell. "Your mate."

"Yes." Miranda nods. Her wing lifts just enough to offer Oliver a view of the other birds without making his presence too obvious. "Evan used to belong to a huge colony. He's been places. His stories are amazing."

"You don't want to come back," Oliver half-muses. "You want to stay here."

"Of course." Miranda pulls herself higher, dropping the wing as she does to keep Oliver veiled. Hidden from her new friends and her mate.

Faintly, he hears the crows laughing. Far off. Somewhere overhead.

"You shouldn't stay here, though," Miranda continues. "You're not a bird, Oliver. You don't belong here any more than I belong in a turtle pen."

"Tortoise." He says it automatically, robotically.

"Whatever." Miranda ripples, a full body dismissal of his presence, his adoration, and his existence.

She fluffs her feathers once, shakes them flat again, and whispers, "Goodbye, Oliver," before strutting away.

Her long legs stab each step into the marshy grass like an arrow striking deep into a turtle's heart.

RAINRIVER ZOOLOGICAL GARDENS

MEMO TO ALL EMPLOYEES

THIS IS A REMINDER TO ALL ZOO STAFF NOT TO PROVIDE ANY FOOD TO THE ANIMALS THAT IS NOT A PART OF THEIR REGULARLY SCHEDULED DIET.

EACH AND EVERY RAINRIVER ANIMAL'S DIET IS OVERSEEN BY A TEAM OF VETERINARIANS AND KEEPERS AND ADDING ANYTHING TO THAT REGIMEN CAN BE DETRIMENTAL TO THE ANIMAL'S HEALTH AND WELL-BEING.

THERE ARE TO BE NO EXCEPTIONS TO THIS RULE.

WE WILL CONSIDER PROVIDING OUTSIDE TREATS TO THE ANIMALS A FIRST TIME FIRING OFFENSE, AS PER EMPLOYEE CONTRACTS.

WE CANNOT ALLOW THE ENTHUSIASM AND EXCITEMENT FOR OUR THRIVING ZOO TO RESULT IN LAX CARE OR DANGEROUS BEHAVIOR.

THIS WILL BE YOUR ONLY WARNING.

REMINDER: THE POTLUCK WILL BE HELD TOMORROW EVENING. DUE TO A CHANGE IN EMPLOYMENT, WE COULD USE ONE MORE PERSON TO BRING A SALAD.

—ZOO MANAGEMENT

Ape House

There are no beans on the ledge today. Gonzo stares at the empty shelf outside his bars as if he can will them into being. While the troop dines, he continues to check every second breath or so, but no cherries magically appear for him.

His need pulls back his lips. He snarls at the melon in his paws.

He-who-sweeps has not come. Instead, a new one drags her broom across the aisle. Her head is down, focused on the work and oblivious to a monkey's expectations. They-who-bring-food do not even carry the paper cups today.

He smells nothing but fruit and macaque feces, and that lack enrages him.

His paws quake until he wraps them around the bars, dragging at the metal as if he might tear it free of its rigidity.

Gonzo screeches. He hops and bares his fangs while They-who-bring-food watch, shaking their heads and discussing him with barking voices.

Gonzo flings shit at them. He loosens his grip on the cage and finds a fresh, filthy pile to grab and toss. To splatter and spray.

They-who-bring-food step out of range, continue their discussion while Gonzo's mind implodes. He must have the cherries. He must taste the bean. He must have, must have, must chew it again or he is certain he will die.

Pigeon Paradise

Peg has grown as fat as a plump, round chicken. She has spent days stuffing herself on birdseed, on little chunks of fruit and flat, striped sunflower seeds. She waddles beside the phony creek at the bottom of the aviary, and she puffs her feathers, becoming a gray sphere as she glowers at the sparkling water.

It is always wet in here.

Her feathers have not dried once since she's arrived. Her eyes swivel and blink against the moist air and her hocks have begun to complain about the extra weight. The aviary birds are not pigeons. They are too crowded, and fight the proximity by keeping to themselves, not gossiping.

There is nothing, really, to whisper about here. Only warm air, shining leaves, and a steady supply of healthy foods.

Peg is miserable.

She scratches at the moist ground, and it clings to her feet, clogging her toes, making her shake and stamp.

There are no cast-off hot dogs here. There is no soft bread, no popcorn, and no soda, and no need at all to fight and squabble over a meal.

She has taken to watching the doors, standing just inside the twin portals while they open, close, open. But she is too fat now, too slow to risk an exit.

Grizzly Grotto

Hector wakes pain-free for the first time in years. He has missed his artist while away, and this new, fresh feeling in his limbs presses him to move quickly. Out of the den, he ambles, hump swaying from side to side between his shoulder blades.

There are not doctors to give him grapes and needles today, but here is his own territory, his fallen log, his trench, and his jagged scratching stump.

It is early, so he indulges in a good, long session with his shaggy back pressed up against the bark. Up and down, Hector wiggles, reaching those persistent itches that his new range of motion finally allows him to assuage.

When he is satisfied, tingling from neck to fat bottom, Hector lifts his muzzle and sniffs. His nose twists left and right, chasing the aroma of his breakfast.

A pile of fruit waits behind the fallen log. It is still early. He sits and pokes his nose among the soft chunks. He noses through colored morsels, and he smells something not unlike the odor which clings perpetually to his doctors.

His first bite is bitter. He thinks the fruit has gone bad, tosses it off, and grabs a new bit. The sharp taste clings to it as if painted on.

Hector's stomach urges him to push past it. He lips cautiously, however, cringing from the unpleasantness hiding behind his breakfast. He remembers sweet grapes on a long skewer. The zoo will open soon. He has wasted his advantage poking at his food and decides to leave it be.

Despite his belly's complaints, he moves back to the stump to wait. He tries a few poses in preparation, testing his new flexibility and striking more than one mighty figure.

She will be impressed, he thinks, to see him stretch so tall, bend so low, and twist...

Hector hears feet upon the paths. Voices sing like birdsong on the morning air. He stands without wavering, gazes over the railing, proud and proper.

His artist is the first face at the rail. Hector greets her with a churr he has perfected on the doctors. She smiles and claps. She reaches into her bag while Hector switches his pose. She pulls something free, something that is not made of art, not a sketchbook, nor a stub of charcoal.

Hector's artist aims the thing at him, shamelessly, and he drops to all fours.

He huffs as the click echoes through his morning, bitter as his fruit, loud as gunfire.

Hector turns, shows the artist his back, and pouts.

There will be nothing more between them.

She has stooped to photography.

Hyena Pen

Alice hates Rocko. He is too large, too clumsy. His breathing scratches like a flea behind her ears. He pants too freely, splashes her water across the cage floor while drinking, and sneaks to the top tier to crowd her while she sleeps.

They have mated twice, and she is done with him.

She paces near the front of the cage, measuring the steps down and back in an abstract fashion and with a growing sense that there simply is no room for him.

Not enough space for two in her box. Not enough room for a Rocko mate.

He cackles from a low tier on the stair-step rock, pants and licks and makes a stupid, lolling face at her. He will want to mate again soon, and Alice thinks she will not let him.

She thinks the cage is too small, the walls too close.

They seem to move as she watches, creeping as Alice stares, one inch closer. Shrinking, boxing, trapping her inside them with a massive, dopey excuse for a male hyena.

Tortoise Trapped

Oliver doesn't hide when the sun rises. He drifts along the marshland pathway, keeping to the far end, away from the herons, and waits to be caught.

The nets arch overhead, a mesh of pale lines that seem to weigh more today. He is pinned by them, held in his dismay by an ephemeral wall.

Eventually, he stops moving. There is nowhere to go, no path that won't eventually lead him back to Miranda. Even with the huge duck pond between them, Oliver imagines he can hear her voice.

It is only the crows laughing, but he hears it in the haughty, clipped tones of a heron who never wanted him to begin with. Oliver tucks his head into his shell and remembers Shanti's voice, deep and encouraging, awed by his shell and his pattern.

He has no reason to think of the elephant now, but the memory soothes him anyway. At least until the crows begin to shout and taunt him again.

Oliver hates them, hates all birds today, but it is an abstract, force-less feeling. His rage has no power. Even Debra is a wisp of irritation only.

The crow didn't trick him, after all. Oliver did this to himself. He knows it, knows he was blind on purpose, willfully deaf to Miranda's indifference. He was obsessed, irrational, unwanted from the start.

It is that which burns brightest now. Not the sting of heartbreak or the raw chafing of rejection. It is shame.

His sense of self has been shattered by the blow to his ego. Oliver feels it seeping in through the gaps in his shell. He was wrong. He was deeply, embarrassingly *wrong*, and how his crimes are exposed.

He is a cracked egg, leaking his flaws onto the path for all to see.

And, overhead, the crows have every right to mock him.

The Crow

The tortoise takes his heartbreak far too well. Debra watches, laughs when the snooty bird rejects him, but her joke is flat. She has to explain the story to the murder three times before they get it and join in.

They follow Oliver for only a short while, taunting and earning no response from their moping victim. It is enough of a game to please the murder, but they are not as impressed with Debra as she desires.

Even devastated, Oliver is ponderous and unexciting.

Debra leaves the marshland to the murder and circles the family farm. A cow is moaning over some mild stomach distress, but it is not worth landing to mock her. She flies to the hyenas, but ever since the male was stuffed into the cage, the female has turned aggressive, more dangerous than usual. Debra will wait until he is removed to find sport there.

She gives up and spends the day in the top of a tall tree, sleeping off her long night setting up Oliver's misery. Maybe he will try again with the heron, but Debra thinks she has gone too far this time. He is too broken to wring any more distress from his situation.

A restless feeling has gripped her, a sense of dread building. Normally, this would please her, but something is not right. Something deep inside her knows fear. As if her sport has left her hollow.

She tucks her beak beneath one wing and lets the zoo fade. In her dreams a dark paw reaches for her. She is caught, captured, stuck in a gage. And only madness circles the skies above her.

She wakes to the sound of human voices.

Night has fallen, and yet the people have not left. It is not quiet. It is not even truly dark. Lights bounce and flicker around the snack bar, and Debra chases them. She sweeps down from the tree and crosses the shadows in between to investigate.

They-who-keep-cages-locked are here. For a moment, Debra believes there will be a hunt. Those-who-carry-guns are with them, and her heart skips merrily. But no. They-who-sweep and They-who-bring-food are also here. They mingle freely with Those-who-pick-up-poop-and-trash.

There are others, too, strangers who join the familiar faces. Their voices raise and chatter. The night fills with the cacophony of their conversation. After hours. This has never happened before.

There is food, too, great piles of it lined up on the outdoor tables.

Debra dives in and steals a flat, round cracker. As she escapes with it, the pigeons, who have swarmed the event, shout obscenities at her. Their whole flock waddles beneath and between the tables, dancing around the many feet—boots and shoes and tall spike-heeled platforms that would skewer a bird if it moved too slowly.

Debra watches in case it happens, but the people in the shoes are foolish. They may be sick, even, and she fears for a moment that the food has been poisoned. They-who-work-at-the-zoo limp and stagger. They bump into one another, shaking, moving as if their legs are not their own.

Like a newborn giraffe trying to stand for the first time.

If they *are* poisoned, they do not suffer. Debra cringes from their laughter, the barking of their brusque, abrasive voices. They are happy. They are masters at the game Debra only plays at. At trapping and at torture. She is among the cruel and the vindictive, the keepers and the punishers. The stealers of freedom.

Debra can do nothing but admire them.

She still feels a disaster brewing. The air is thick with it. This mob of humans, the pigeons cursing and squabbling underfoot, the poisoned food and drink. A new tension crackles on the air. It has, she realizes, been brewing all along. Something terrible is about to happen. Debra feels it like a storm coming, and she lets her dark heart fill with anticipation again.

The danger sings to her. Its voice is tragedy. Its words are a promise of disaster. Debra perches on a light post, high above the party, and waits for the lightning to strike.

See parts I-V of Frances Pauli's story "The Zoo Diaries V" online at Metaphorosis.
If you like them, leave a comment. Authors love that!
Remember to subscribe to our e-mail updates so you'll know when new stories are posted.

Copyright

Title information

Metaphorosis May 2023

ISSN: 2573-136X (online)
ISBN: 978-1-64076-257-2 (e-book)
ISBN: 978-1-64076-258-9 (paperback)

Works of fiction

This book contains works of fiction. Characters, dialogue, places, organizations, incidents, and events portrayed in the works are fictional and are products of the author's imagination or used fictitiously. Any resemblance to actual persons, places, organizations, or events is coincidental.

All rights reserved

Moral rights asserted

Each author whose work is included in this book has asserted their moral rights, including the right to be identified as the author of their respective work(s).

Publisher

Metaphorosis
a magazine of speculative fiction

Metaphorosis Magazine is an imprint of
Metaphorosis Publishing
Neskowin, OR, USA

www.metaphorosis.com

"Metaphorosis" is a registered trademark.

Discounts available

Substantial discounts are available for educational institutions, including writing workshops. Discounts are also available for quantity purchases. For details, contact Metaphorosis at metaphorosis.com/about

Metaphorosis Publishing

Metaphorosis offers beautifully written science fiction and fantasy. Our imprints include:

Metaphorosis Magazine
Plant Based Press
Verdage
Vestige

You can also find us:
@Metaphorosis
@Metaphorosis@writing.exchange
www.facebook.com/metaphorosis

Help keep Metaphorosis running by supporting us at
Patreon.com/metaphorosis

See more about some of our books on the following pages.

Metaphorosis
a magazine of speculative fiction

Metaphorosis is an online speculative fiction magazine dedicated to quality writing. We publish an original story every week, along with author bios, interviews, and notes on story origins.

We also publish monthly print and e-book issues, as well as yearly Best of and Complete anthologies.

Come and see us online at magazine.Metaphorosis.com.

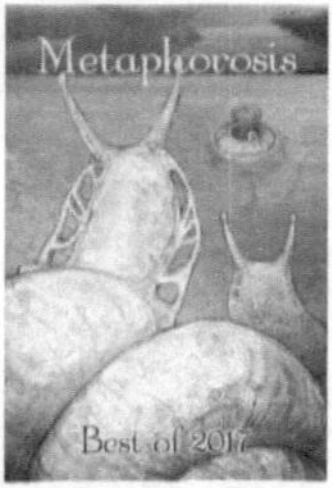

Plant Based Press

Vegan-friendly science fiction and fantasy, including anthologies of the year's best SFF stories, from 2016-2020.

Chambers of the Heart

speculative stories
by
B. Morris Allen

A heart that's a building, a dog that's a program, a woman sinking irretrievably — stories about love, loss, and motion.

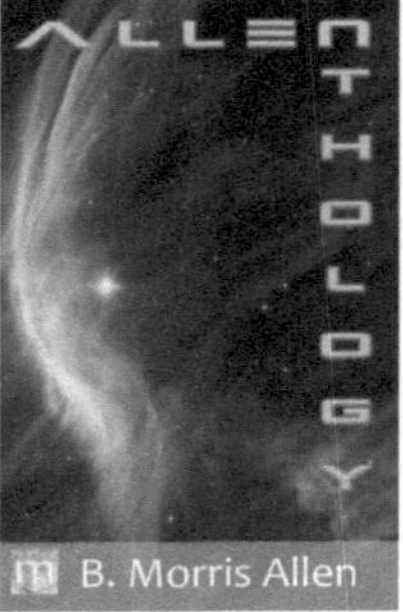

Susurrus

A darkly romantic story of magic, love, and suffering.

Allenthology: Volume I

Including three full collections of SFF stories.

Verdage

Science fiction and fantasy books for writers — full of great stories, often with an additional focus on the craft of speculative fiction writing.

Reading 5X5 x3

Changes

How do stories move from 'maybe' to published?

Here are 15 case studies of stories published in *Metaphorosis* magazine.

Reading 5X5 x2

Duets

How do authors' voices change when they collaborate?

A round-robin of five talented science fiction and fantasy authors collaborating with each other and writing solo.

Including stories by Evan Marcroft, David Gallay, J. Tynan Burke, L'Erin Ogle, and Douglas Anstruther.

Score

an SFF symphony

An anthology with an emotional score from the heights of joy to the depths of despair – but always with a little hope shining through.

Reading 5X5

Five stories, five times

See how different writers take on the same material.

Reading 5X5

Writers' Edition

Two extra stories, the story seed, and authors' notes on writing.

Vestige

Vestige

Novelettes, novellas, and novels by Metaphorosis authors.

The Nocturnals
Mariah Montoya

Night is Dangerous. Day is deadly.

Where day and night last thirty years, humans move constantly stay ahead of the night and cruel Nocturnals that call it home. But a boy is lost out there.

9 781640 762589